Teggs is no ordinary dinosaur –
he's an **ASTROSAUR!** Captain of
the amazing spaceship DSS *Sauropod*,
he goes on dangerous missions and
fights evil – along with his faithful
crew, Gipsy, Arx and Iggy!

For more astro-fun visit the website
www.astrosaurs.co.uk

Read all the adventures of
Teggs, Gipsy, Arx and Iggy!

RIDDLE OF THE RAPTORS

THE HATCHING HORROR

THE SEAS OF DOOM

THE MIND-SWAP MENACE

THE SKIES OF FEAR

THE SPACE GHOSTS

DAY OF THE DINO-DROIDS

THE TERROR-BIRD TRAP

TEETH OF THE T.RE
(specially published for
World Book Day 2007)

THE STAR PIRATES

THE CLAWS OF CHRISTMAS

Find out more at www.astrosaurs.co.uk

TEGGS'
TRIPLE-SAURUS

Steve Cole

Illustrated by
Charlie Fowkes and Woody Fox

RED FOX

TEGGS' TRIPLE-SAURUS
A RED FOX BOOK 978 1 862 30592 2

This collection first published exclusively for W H Smith in Great Britain by Red Fox,
an imprint of Random House Children's Books
A Random House Group Company

Collection copyright © Steve Cole, 2007

1 3 5 7 9 10 8 6 4 2

RIDDLE OF THE RAPTORS
First published in Great Britain by Red Fox, 2005

Copyright © Steve Cole, 2005
Illustrations copyright © Charlie Fowkes, 2005

THE SEAS OF DOOM
First published in Great Britain by Red Fox, 2005

Copyright © Steve Cole, 2005
Cover illustration and map © Charlie Fowkes, 2005
Illustrations copyright © Woody Fox, 2005

THE SKIES OF FEAR
First published in Great Britain by Red Fox, 2006

Copyright © Steve Cole, 2006
Cover illustration © Steve Richards/Dynamo Design
Illustrations copyright © Woody Fox, 2006

The Random House Group Limited supports The Forest Stewardship Council (FSC), the
leading international forest certification organisation. All out titles that are printed on
Greenpeace approved FSC certified paper carry the FSC logo. Our paper procurement
policy can be found at: www.rbooks.co.uk/environment

Set in Bembo Schoolbook

Mixed Sources
Product group from well-managed
forests and other controlled sources
www.fsc.org Cert no. TT-COC-2139
© 1996 Forest Stewardship Council

Red Fox Books are published by Random House Children's Books,
61–63 Uxbridge Road, London W5 5SA

www.kidsatrandomhouse.co.uk
www.rbooks.co.uk

Addresses for companies within The Random House Group Limited can be found at:
www.randomhouse.co.uk/offices.htm

THE RANDOM HOUSE GROUP Limited Reg. No. 954009

A CIP catalogue record for this book is available from the British Library.

Printed in the UK by CPI Bookmarque, Croydon CR0 4TD

WARNING!

THINK YOU KNOW ABOUT DINOSAURS?

THINK AGAIN!

The dinosaurs . . .

Big, stupid, lumbering reptiles. Right?

All they did was eat, sleep and roar a bit. Right?

Died out millions of years ago when a big meteor struck the Earth. Right?

Wrong!

The dinosaurs weren't stupid. They may have had small brains, but they used them well. They had big thoughts and big dreams.

By the time the meteor hit, the last dinosaurs had already left Earth for ever. Some breeds had discovered how to travel through space as early as the Triassic period, and were already enjoying a new life among the stars.

No one has found evidence of dinosaur technology yet. But the first fossil bones were only unearthed in 1822, and new finds are being made all the time. The proof is out there, buried in the ground.

And the dinosaurs live on, way out in space, even now. They've settled down in a place they call the Jurassic Quadrant and over the last sixty-five million years they've gone on evolving . . .

The dinosaurs we'll be meeting are

 part of a special group called the Dinosaur Space Service. These heroic herbivores are not just dinosaurs.

They are *astrosaurs!*

NOTE: The following story has been translated from secret Dinosaur Space Service records. Earthling dinosaur names are used throughout, although some changes have been made for easy reading. There's even a guide to help you pronounce the dinosaur names at the back of the book.

THE CREW OF THE
DSS SAUROPOD

**CAPTAIN
TEGGS STEGOSAUR**

ARX ORANO,
FIRST OFFICER

GIPSY SAURINE,
COMMUNICATIONS
OFFICER

IGGY TOOTH,
CHIEF ENGINEER

Jurassic Quadrant

Ankylos

Steggos

Diplox

INDEPENDE[NT]
DINOSAUR
ALLIANCE

vegetarian
sector

Squawk
Major

DSS
UNION OF
PLANETS

PTEROSAURIA

Tri System

Corytho

Lambeos

Cryp[t]

Iguanos

Aqua Minor

SEA RE

OUTER SPACE

Geldos Cluster

Teerex Major

T Olympus

TYRANNOSAUR
TERRITORIES

Planet Sixty

carnivore
sector

Raptos

THEROPOD EMPIRE

Megalos

os

vegmeat
zone
(neutral space)

PTILE SPACE

Pliosaur
Nurseries

Not to scale

RIDDLE
OF THE
RAPTORS

By Steve Cole

Illustrated by
Charlie Fowkes

For Tobey

Chapter One

THE ADVENTURE BEGINS

Space. It stretched on for ever.

Distant stars twinkled. Comets showed off their sparkling tails. Strange planets hung like bright bulbs in the black sky.

Teggs Stegosaur stared out at it all in wonder. He was standing on the top deck of a massive space station – the headquarters of the Dinosaur Space Service.

At last, he thought. After years of training, I've made it. I'm an *astrosaur*! He frowned. But why have I been asked to come to headquarters alone? I hope I haven't messed up already!

Just then, a small pterosaur flapped noisily down the corridor towards him. "Admiral Rosso will see you now," it squawked. "Follow me! Follow me!"

Teggs gulped, and lumbered after the flying reptile on his four squat, scaly

legs. He was a handsome, orange-brown stegosaurus, eight metres long from the point of his beak to the tip of his spiny tail. A line of armoured plates ran down his scaly back like a dozen small sails.

The pterosaur perched just outside the admiral's office. "In you go," it screeched. "In you go!"

Teggs pushed through the heavy jungle vines that hung down over the doorway. The floor was thick with juicy moss, and the walls were bright with flowers and fruits. Here and there, tall, thick tree trunks stretched up to the high grassy ceiling. Astrosaurs always kept plenty of plants around the place, and not just because they were good to eat. Their spaceships ran on dung, so every meal meant a little more fuel for the engines.

"Ah! Young Teggs!" boomed Admiral Rosso from behind a vast wooden desk.

He was the crusty old barosaurus in charge of the Dinosaur Space Service. "Thank you for coming."

Teggs carefully raised his front legs in a dinosaur salute. "You wanted to see me, sir?"

"I wanted to congratulate you," smiled the admiral. His scaly head bobbed about on a neck as long as a fireman's hose – and ten times thicker. "You have passed your final Space Service tests with a record-breaking score. You are without doubt the bravest, most daring – and *hungriest* astrosaur ever to train here."

Teggs blushed and quickly swallowed the mouthful of ferns he'd pulled from the floor. "Thank you, sir. Er, sorry for eating your office, sir."

"Nothing wrong with a hearty appetite," the admiral chuckled. "But I think it's *adventure* you're truly hungry for."

Teggs grinned. "My stomach's rumbling at the thought of it!"

"That's why I'm putting you in charge of your very own spaceship," said the admiral. "I'm making you a captain!"

"Captain? And my very own spaceship?" Teggs's beak dropped open in amazement. This was a dream come true!

The admiral pulled aside a curtain of jungle creepers to reveal a window. Through it, Teggs saw an amazing spaceship. It was shaped like an enormous egg, with six thick prongs sticking out. At the end of every prong sat a slightly smaller egg. Teggs supposed these were the shuttles.

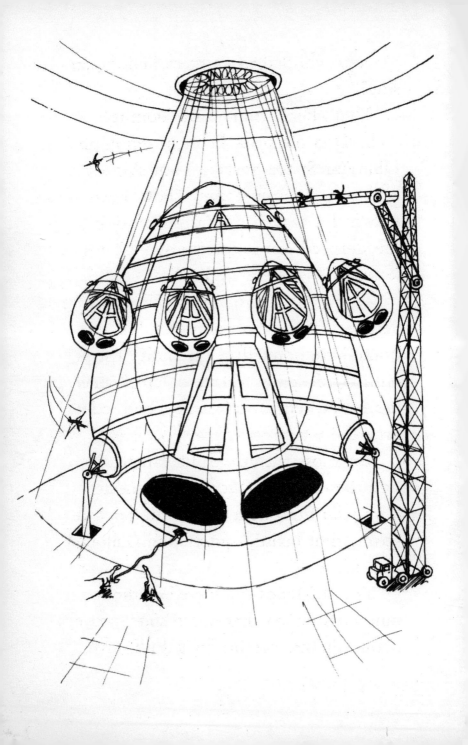

Teggs whistled in wonder. "That's *my* ship?"

"That's her," beamed the admiral. "The DSS *Sauropod*, finest in the entire Dinosaur Space Service. That ship – and you, Captain Teggs – have been chosen for a very important mission." He unrolled some star charts with his long tail. "Recognize this?"

"That's the Jurassic Quadrant," said Teggs. "The part of space we call home." He pointed to one half of it with a tail spike. "Those green planets are in the Vegetarian Sector. The red ones are where the carnivores live."

"Yes, those mean old meat-eaters," said the admiral. "We've all come a long way from dear old Earth. Such a shame that beastly space rock walloped into it."

"Yes, sir." Teggs shuddered. If the dinosaurs hadn't discovered space travel before the meteor hit, they'd all have been wiped out! "Do you think anyone will ever live on Earth again, sir?"

"Who knows?" sighed the admiral. "But we dinosaurs have thrived in outer space. Earth is just a titchy speck compared to the vastness of the Jurassic Quadrant!"

Teggs nodded keenly. "And there's still so much of it to explore!"

"That's where you come in," said the admiral. "You're now a fully trained astrosaur captain. Your mission is to explore space in the DSS *Sauropod*. To go in peace . . . To spread the way of the plant-eater . . . To keep an eye on those greedy meat-eaters . . . And to protect our people, wherever they may be."

Teggs nodded even *more* keenly. "I'll need a crew," he said.

"I've already got you one." The admiral swatted a button on the wall with his tail, and the window turned

into a scanner screen.
It showed a picture of
a green triceratops
with three proud horns
and a parrot-like beak.

"This is Arx Orano,"
said the admiral. "He's
a very well respected
astrosaur. He'll be your first officer."

Teggs smiled. Then the image changed
to show a pretty duck-billed dinosaur,
striped all over.

"This is your communications officer,
Gipsy Saurine," said the admiral. "You
can see from her snout that she's a

hadrosaur. Her
mind's as sharp as
a raptor's claw and
she loves a
challenge." He
smiled. "That's
why I've put her
on *your* ship!"

"I'm glad to have her on board," said Teggs.

The picture changed again. Now it showed a tough looking iguanodon on his hind legs. His arms were thick and strong.

"And this is Iggy Tooth," said the admiral. "A top engineer. He can turn a clawful of scrap into a space motor before you can say 'ornithomimosaur'."

Teggs gulped. He wasn't sure if he could say that at all.

"He's also very good in battle," the admiral said. "So if you ever find trouble – find Iggy fast!"

"I will," said Teggs grimly.

"So, when am I off on these exciting missions?"

"Oh, soon. Very soon." The admiral cleared his throat. "But there's a little something I need you to do first . . ."

Chapter Two

BATTLE STATIONS!

"A taxi service!" huffed Captain Teggs for the hundredth time. "The finest ship in the fleet, the best crew . . . and the admiral turns us into a taxi service!"

Gipsy turned her long, flat snout towards him. "Not just *any* taxi service, Captain," she reminded him. "We're in charge of the Vegetarian Sector's top athletes. We'll get them to the Great Dinosaur Games in style!"

Arx nodded his frilly head. "It's the biggest space sports

14

contest *ever*. Every race in the quadrant is coming to Olympus for the games. And when those miserable meat-eaters see the DSS *Sauropod* arrive, think how impressed they'll be!"

"I suppose so." Teggs chewed grumpily on some ferns from the wall of his control pit. "How long before we arrive?"

"Right now, we're just passing the moons of Minnos," said Gipsy. "That's the halfway point. Then, once we've swung round Planet Sixty, it's straight on to Olympus. We should arrive tomorrow night."

"The games start the day after!" Arx added.

"And nothing to do until then," sighed Teggs. "I was hoping for a little more action—"

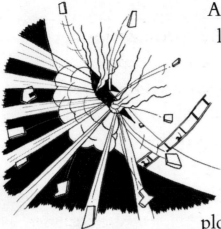

A split-second later – *Ka-Boom!* The whole ship shook with an enormous explosion. Teggs spat out his beakful of plants and jumped up from the control pit. "What was *that*?" he bellowed.

"Warning! Warning!" The shriek of the alarm pterosaur echoed out from every speaker on the ship. "Unknown invaders coming aboard!"

Arx swung his great head round to his instruments. "Someone's blown a hole in our ship!"

"On our first ever flight?" cried Gipsy. "That's not fair!"

"I wanted action," Teggs muttered.

"And I guess I've got it!"

"Red alert!" The alarm pterosaur squawked even louder. "Raptors on board! Repeat — *raptors on board!*"

"Battle stations!" Teggs roared. "Gipsy, where *are* these raptors?"

"The hole's on level seven, Captain," Gipsy reported. "It's close to the relaxation room." Then the crest of her scaly face flushed bright blue with worry. "Uh-oh. That's where the athletes are!"

"We have to drive these raptors off the ship — *fast*," said Teggs. "Arx, get Iggy on to it!"

Arx jabbed the communicator with his nose horn. "Iggy!" he snapped. "Raptor invaders on level seven. Our athletes are in danger. Prepare for battle!"

"Switch on the scanners, Gipsy," Teggs ordered.

At first they could only see the rocky

moons of Minnos. Then a sinister craft came into view, hanging in space like a giant ivory tooth.

"A raptor death-ship!" cried Gipsy. "We've flown into an ambush!"

Suddenly another big explosion sent the *Sauropod* spinning. Teggs's seven-ton body was rolled over and over until he smashed into the thick plant-life that covered the nearest wall. His team of tiny flying reptiles – fifty daring dimorphodon – flapped wildly about the flight deck, trying to sort out the damage. They bashed the controls with their beaks and yanked on levers with tough, bony claws.

Arx rose from the grassy floor and checked his instruments. "There are *five* death-ships out there! They were hiding behind the moons. Now we're surrounded!"

"Put up the shields!" Teggs yelled. "And fetch me my armour!"

The dimorphodon crew rushed to obey. In moments, three of the flapping reptiles were fitting Teggs into his head and tail armour. "I'll join the fight with Iggy down below," he said. "Arx, Gipsy, try to get us out of here."

"Understood, Captain," barked Arx. The dimorphodon team leaders flapped down to perch on his head, ready to take his commands.

Gipsy looked at Teggs. "Be careful, sir," she said.

★

As the moss-lined lift heaved down to the crew decks, Teggs heard the sound of fighting grow louder. As the lift reached the seventh floor, he gritted his teeth. The spines that ran along his arched back turned a deep, warning red.

"I'll get those raptors," he muttered fiercely. "They'll be sorry they stepped onto *my* ship!"

As the doors opened Teggs sprang out, flexed the great, spiked club of his armoured tail, then charged along the corridor.

He found the battle raging ahead of him. The air was thick with shrieks and roars. Nimble velociraptors in full battle armour skipped around the heavier ankylosaurs blocking their way. A dozen iguanodon reared up on their hind legs, roaring. Their claws ended in metal tips that fired stun rays into the raptor ranks. The beams of light bounced off the raptors' chestplates and helmets. Teggs's ears rang with *thwacks* and *thuds* as his crew's heavy tails swiped through the air at their attackers.

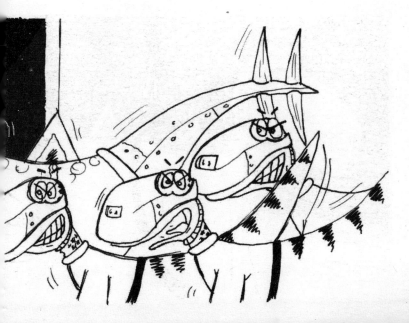

Iggy Tooth was in the thick of the fighting. He caught sight of Teggs and swiftly saluted. "Set your stun claws to maximum, boys!" he cried, a blur of green scales as he dodged his way through the fighting, keeping perfect balance with his short, stiff tail. "The captain's come to join us! We can't lose now!"

But even as he spoke, two raptors finally managed to tear their way straight past the massive ankylosaur that barred their way. They bared their blood-red teeth at Teggs.

"Sssurrender your ship, Captain," hissed the largest of the two raptors as they advanced with razor-sharp claws. "Or you shall die!"

Chapter Three

KIDNAP!

Teggs shook his head and sneered at the approaching raptors. "I'm not ready to become a stego-burger just yet," he growled. "And it'll take more than a couple of corny carnivores like you to take my ship!"

With that, Teggs lashed out with his armoured tail and sent the first raptor flying. The second brought its jaws down hard on the spiky, bone-like club at the tail's end.

It was a bad move. A second later, every tooth in its ugly head was broken and tinkling down to the mossy floor.

The furious carnivore gnashed its gums and turned to its fallen mate. "Ssstop him!"

The first raptor leaped forward once more to bite Teggs on the neck. Teggs quickly ducked down and turned with surprising speed, so that his attacker smacked into his back. The raptor toppled backwards and landed on top of its friend.

Teggs prepared to fight his way

through to Iggy. But then a strange wailing noise started up. At once, the raptors broke off from the battle and backed off.

"You hear that, boys?" cried Iggy triumphantly. "That's the raptor retreat signal! They're giving up! Come on, let's see them off the ship!"

As Iggy's battle squad charged off after the retreating raptors, Teggs pressed his head up against the communicator. "Captain to flight deck. Well done, crew. We've scared them off! The raptors are running away!"

But Arx sounded worried. "I don't think we *did* scare them off, Captain," he said. "We only fired off two laser bolts, and the raptor ships didn't even fire back."

Teggs thought hard. "You know, you might be right," he said slowly. "Those soldiers gave up pretty easily too. One minute they wanted me to surrender the *Sauropod* – the next they were retreating back to their ship as fast as their claws would carry them."

Gipsy's voice sounded over the speaker. "Perhaps they only retreated because they'd got what they came for . . ."

"Of course!" Teggs grunted and charged off down the corridor after Iggy. The raptors didn't really want to take the ship at all. They started the fight just to keep Teggs and his crew busy – while they went after the athletes . . .

"They must be planning to ruin the Great Dinosaur Games!" he cried. "But surely they wouldn't *dare* eat our greatest athletes!"

Teggs charged into the *Sauropod's* enormous relaxation room. It was like a miniature forest, with a crystal clear bathing pool in its centre. Ordinarily the dinosaur athletes would've been chewing and resting or splashing about. But right now they were all cowering behind a large saltasaurus wrestler in the corner.

"Are they gone?" whimpered a maiasaura shot-putter, its belly pressed low against the grass so that it could barely be seen.

"Yes, they've gone back to their ship," said Teggs. "I was worried they'd taken all of you with them!"

"No way," said the saltasaurus, the bumps on its hide bristling. "Two raptors looked in here, but I scared them off."

"I see," said Teggs doubtfully. He knew that raptors didn't scare easily. "Is anyone missing?"

"Wait! The stegoceras aren't here," cried the shot-putter. "They were in the shower when the alarms sounded."

"Oh no!" Teggs groaned. He charged back down the corridor and through the shower doors. Then he stuck his head inside. "Anyone there?" he asked as he peered through the steam.

But his only answer was the mournful drip of water on to the floor. There was no sign of the stegoceras athletes. The showers were empty.

Teggs stomped back to the communicator in the wall. "Captain to flight deck," he growled. "You were right, Arx. This wasn't just a raid. It was a *kidnapping!*"

Chapter Four

A DEADLY MESSAGE

Captain Teggs sat tensely in his control pit, chewing on twigs.

Arx had found images of the two stegoceras and Gipsy had put them on the scanner. The athletes were perky orange creatures, each about the size of a goat. One was named Hank, the other Crank. They had feeble forearms, long, straight tails and ran

about on two legs. But their heads were truly eye-catching: a solid lump of

bone the size of a football bulged above their snouts.

"What sport do they play?" wondered Gipsy.

"They were hot tips to win the head-butting contest," Arx said.

"I'm an idiot!" sighed Teggs. "Two days to go until the Great Dinosaur Games, and I let a bunch of raptors sneak on board and take our best butters. I must have a brain the size of a ping-pong ball!"

Arx cleared his throat. "Er, you *do* have a brain the size of a ping-pong ball, Captain," he said delicately. "You know, being a stegosaurus and all."

"So I do!" said Teggs, cheering up a bit. "I shouldn't be so hard on myself."

Just then, Teggs's personal communicator beeped.

"Uh-oh," he said. "Here's someone who *will* be hard on me. It's Admiral Rosso!"

31

"Captain Teggs!" boomed Admiral Rosso. "I've read your report. I can hardly believe what has happened. It's a disaster! A mess! A total foul-up!"

"I'm sorry, sir," said Teggs. "Perhaps . . . perhaps I'm just not good enough to be captain of the *Sauropod*."

"Piffle," said the admiral sternly. "Everyone makes mistakes, Captain. It's how you make up for them that counts." He paused. "Just make sure you sort out *this* mistake fast – before the Great Dinosaur Games begin!"

The communicator switched off.

"Are you all right, Captain?" asked Arx gently.

"Never mind me," said Teggs. "It's those poor stegoceras athletes I'm worried about!"

Gipsy raised her snout in the air and whistled and hooted at the dimorphodon flight crew. A few of them flapped down at once and massaged their captain's spiky back with their claws. "So, what do we do now?" she asked.

Iggy was pacing up and down the

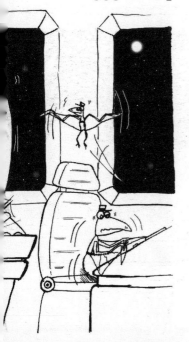

flight deck in a foul temper, clicking his thumb spikes. "I say we hunt down these velociraptor vermin and *make* them give us back our athletes!"

"The Jurassic Quadrant is a big area to search," Arx reminded him.

"Why did they only take the head-butters out of everyone on board?" wondered Gipsy.

"You've got something there!" Teggs rose up suddenly, and the dimorphodon flapped off in fright. "The raptors looked in the athletes' room, but kept searching till they found the stegoceras in the showers. Why?"

"Well, if the raptors *have* taken the stegoceras for a reason," Arx said, "we can only wait and see if they tell us what it is."

There was a sudden creaking, squeaking noise from Gipsy's communications console. "I'm getting a message, Captain. Picture and sound," she reported briskly, checking the readout. "It's from a raptor!"

"Put it on the scanner," Teggs ordered.

The screen showed the hateful features of a big, scaly raptor. Clearly it had been in many battles over the

years. Its pointed jaw was scuffed and scraped, and it wore a black eye-patch over one eye.

"I am General Loki," said the raptor in a silky smooth whisper. "Commander of the Seven Fleets of Death! Ruler of the meat mines of Raptos! Eater of edmontosaurus, devourer of diplodocus—"

"And all-round pain in the tail," Teggs

cut in before the raptor got really
carried away. He had heard of General
Loki – the nastiest, meanest velociraptor
in the Jurassic Quadrant. "At least
you've got less of a lisp than your
raptor crew. What do you want?"

Loki narrowed his one remaining eye.
"It's what *you* want that we should be
discussing, Captain Teggs . . ." Loki
moved aside from the scanner cameras
to reveal the two stegoceras athletes
hunched up behind him. Both of them
had grubby bandages wrapped round
their heads.

"Hank! Crank!" Teggs reared up out

of his control pit. "Are you OK?"

"We're cool!" Hank and Crank chorused, and lightly tapped their heads together as if to prove it. "Ouch!" they both yelled.

Gipsy frowned. "Have the raptors hurt you?"

"Nah," said Hank. "We just woke up with a headache." He waved his feeble forearm at his bandage. "Look! Some raptor doctors checked us out, then gave us these headbands!"

Crank nodded enthusiastically. "Cool or what!"

The stegoceras were about to bash heads again when two raptor guards restrained them.

Loki came back into view. "So you see, Captain," he said. "Your athletes are fit and well. And they'll stay that way if you agree to our terms."

Teggs glared at him. "And just what exactly *are* your terms?"

"You must pay us a billion pieces of purest gold!" Loki laughed nastily. "And if you refuse, *your* athletes become *my* supper!"

Chapter Five

SHOWDOWN ON PLANET SIXTY

Iggy, Arx, Teggs and Gipsy stared at each other in disbelief.

"A billion pieces?" Teggs spluttered. "You're crazy! It would take *years* to gather all that gold!"

"Oh. Really?" Loki looked a little downcast, and clicked his claws. "All right then . . . call it twenty."

"Twenty?" echoed Teggs.

Loki nodded. "But throw in a nice flat-screen satellite monitor too. Mine's just broken."

Iggy, Arx, Teggs and Gipsy stared at each other once again, in still *deeper* disbelief.

"From a billion pieces . . . to twenty?" Teggs started counting on his toes, then frowned. "That *is* quite a drop — isn't it?"

"Raptors are totally rubbish at doing deals, Captain," Arx said in a low voice. "They normally sort out any squabbles by biting each other."

"Mind you," said Iggy grudgingly, "that Loki's smarter than he looks. Those flat-screen satellite monitors are brilliant!"

"Oh, and we want some moss too,"

Loki added as if the thought had just occurred to him. "It goes so well with raw apatosaurus." He licked his leathery lips with a forked tongue. "The exchange will be made at noon tomorrow on Planet Sixty."

Teggs frowned. "Planet Sixty? Isn't that on the way to Olympus?"

"Yes, Captain," said Arx. "It's a small, swampy planet just outside the Vegetarian Sector. It's so dull, no one could be bothered to name it!"

Loki smiled. "I trust your . . . *flimsy* new ship can reach Planet Sixty in time?"

Teggs narrowed his eyes. "We'll be there."

"Splendid. But no tricks," said the grizzled general. "You're to come unarmed, Captain, with just one member of your crew. Until tomorrow . . ." He nodded his head in farewell, and the screen went blank.

"What do we do, Captain?" asked Gipsy.

"What *can* we do?" Teggs uprooted a fern from the floor and chewed it grumpily. "You heard the admiral. We need to sort this out fast. Next stop, Planet Sixty — full speed ahead!"

And so the *Sauropod* sailed through space towards the pick-up point.

"Planet Sixty is coming into range, Captain," announced Gipsy at last. She blinked her wide eyes at him. "Iggy says the shuttle is ready to depart."

Teggs came out of the control pit. "Those raptors are up to something," he said. "I feel it in my tail spikes."

As he stomped off towards the shuttle, Teggs had an uneasy feeling that something was badly wrong. He felt naked without his electro-tail armour. He bet Iggy felt the same without his stun claws. But Loki had insisted they must come unarmed. Teggs couldn't risk crossing him while the two athletes were prisoners.

Even so – would the raptors keep their side of the bargain?

Iggy saluted Teggs as he came aboard the shuttle. "Dung burners set to maximum, Captain!"

"OK," Teggs nodded. "Blast off!"

The shuttle – shaped like a giant egg with two noisy motors on the fat end – began to shudder and shake as the power began to build. The engines ignited. Soon, the sweet smell of dinosaur manure filled the air as the shuttle thundered away into space.

Within minutes they were flying through the grotty green skies of Planet Sixty. With a slithering bump and a rattling roar, the shuttle skidded to a stop on the swampy surface.

Teggs opened the doors and led the way outside. Iggy waddled close behind him carrying the ransom on his back.

They hadn't walked far before they saw the raptor death shuttle – an

44

enormous, pointed spike with a blood-red tip. Next to it stood General Loki and three of his raptor guards, watching over the athletes with

hungry eyes.

"Welcome, Captain," sneered Loki. He eyed the bundle on Iggy's back. "You have met my demands, I see."

"Let's just get this over with," said Teggs. He swished his enormous tail from side to side menacingly. "Give us back our athletes!"

With a hiss, the raptor guards herded the stegoceras over to Teggs. One of the guards came towards Iggy, its claws raised and ready to slash. It cut clean through the thick twine that bound the ransom bundle to the iguanodon's back and paraded the package back to its ship in triumph.

Teggs peered at the athletes with their bandaged heads. "You two OK?"

"We're cool," said Hank.

"Just glad to be out of that fleapit," added Crank, nodding at the raptor shuttle.

"Farewell, Captain!" called Loki. "Enjoy the Great Dinosaur Games! I'm sure they'll go with a bang!" With a nasty chuckle, he scuttled into his ship, which took off at once.

"Good riddance!" yelled Crank.

"Totally," Hank nodded. "That ship stank of meat, man!" He tried to mime being suffocated, but his little forearms couldn't reach his neck.

"Wait a second," Iggy said gruffly. His nostrils were twitching. "Did either

of you *sit* in any of
that meat?"

Hank and Crank
shook their bandaged
heads.

Teggs sniffed the air,
and wrinkled his snout. "I
can smell it too . . ."

Suddenly the swampy
ground began to shake.
"What's that?" Hank
squeaked.

"Something big," shouted
Iggy, looking around as the pounding
on the ground got louder. "Coming
this way!"

Teggs lumbered up a small hill to see
what it was – and froze in his tracks.

A terrifying creature was bounding
up towards him – a real giant, at least
three times the size of Teggs. It stood
upright on powerful legs as big as tree
trunks. Its massive mouth brimmed

with dagger-like teeth. Hot on its scaly
heels, another ten of the monsters were
approaching fast.

"Back to the ship, quick!" called
Teggs as he thundered back down the
hill. *"There are T. rexes on this planet!"*

Chapter Six

DANGEROUS FLIGHT

Teggs led the charge back to the shuttle.
The ground shook like it was going to
open up beneath their feet.
T. rexes didn't normally hunt in packs –
unless they were scouting out new
planets to take over . . .

"You're welcome to this dump,"
muttered Teggs. Then he skidded to a
halt. Iggy and the others almost
crashed into him.

Another T. rex, the biggest yet, was
looming over their shuttle.

Teggs squared up to the ferocious
carnivore. "Iggy, I'll lead it off. Get
those athletes inside the ship!"

Iggy hesitated. "But, Captain—"

"Do it!" growled Teggs.

He ran to the edge of a cliff, and the T. rex chased after him. Then Teggs faced up to the monster. He swung his tail around so fast that the spikes on the end of it became an ivory blur.

The terrifying tyrannosaur roared and lunged forward, but Teggs's tail whacked it on the side of its head. Staggering sideways in surprise, the T. rex fell over the edge of the cliff and into the swamp below.

But there was no time to celebrate. Teggs rushed back to the shuttle to find the whole snarling gang of T. rexes were now blocking his way.

"This *our* planet," growled their leader. "You in big trouble, plant-boy."

"We were just visiting," Teggs told her. "We'll be off now. Leave you to it."

The T. rex shook its head. "No."

"Er, can't we talk about this?" asked Teggs hopefully, edging towards the shuttle.

"No," it said.

Teggs suddenly remembered what his astrosaur trainer had taught him:

T. rexes hate talking. They've never learned how to do it properly. Ten seconds into a conversation and they usually eat the person they're speaking to.

"We HUNGRY!" roared the T. rex leader. It opened its jaws and lunged at Teggs. He rolled clear just in time — and the creature crunched down on one of the shuttle's motors. Its teeth tore the engine clear off!

"Take off, Iggy!" yelled Teggs. "Never

mind me! With only one engine you'll have a bumpy ride, but you might just make it!"

The T. rex leader roared in anger. The engine was jammed in its mouth! It lumbered towards Teggs and tried to stamp on his tail.

Teggs backed away. "Missed me, loser!" he called bravely. But deep down he knew there was no hope of escape. Already the other tyrannosaurs were drawing closer, roaring and snapping their gruesome jaws . . .

The shuttle still hadn't taken off. Teggs guessed Iggy couldn't bring himself to leave his captain behind.

"Go *now*, Iggy!" he yelled. "That's an order!"

"Aye-aye, Captain," said Iggy sadly.

The shuttle's remaining engine burst into life – and made a *very* rude noise. The T. rexes all turned round in shock.

While they were distracted, Teggs pushed past them. The shuttle doors heaved open and he leaped inside, scattering the stegoceras like scaly skittles.

"Welcome back, Captain!" beamed Iggy.

"You didn't make that dreadful noise, did you?" gasped Teggs, warily sniffing the air.

"Not me!" said Iggy, revving the engine. "There must have been a build-up of dung gas trapped in the exhaust pipe. It's clear now."

Teggs sighed. "If only *we* were clear of these T. rexes . . ."

The shuttle took off wonkily. It was meant to fly with two engines, not one. Unbalanced, it started to spin in all directions.

"Cool!" yelled Hank and Crank happily, as if it was a fairground ride. The shuttle bumped and bounced

against the ground, and soon the ship's
floor was flooded with swamp muck.

"I can't control it!" Iggy shouted.

To Teggs's dismay, the T. rexes were
running after the spinning shuttle.

"They're catching up!" yelled Crank.

The T. rexes
loomed up,
gnashing their
jaws in
triumph – all
except their
leader, who still
had a mouthful
of engine. The
shuttle made
another rude
noise as it dipped down again.

"I know how you feel," muttered
Teggs.

Then, suddenly, his little brain was
filled with a big idea.

"There's just one chance," Teggs cried.

He scavenged through the swamp muck until he found a big, sharp stone. "Try to hold her steady, Iggy!" he yelled. Then he picked up the stone with his beak and tossed it in the air.

With a noise like a whip crack his tail lashed out and struck the stone, sending it flying out through the shuttle's doors.

The stone smacked against the engine caught in the T. rex leader's teeth. With a fiery bang, the engine exploded!

The T. rex fell backwards with an angry roar of pain. And to everyone's amazement, the other T. rexes toppled over too!

Iggy hooted for joy. "What happened, Captain? What did you do?"

"The rude noise reminded me – our engines run on gas made by burning dung," said Teggs. "They're full to bursting with it! And that gas is explosive stuff . . ."

"It sure is!" Iggy grinned. "There's a lot to be said for a good, healthy vegetarian's diet!"

Hank and Crank clapped their tiny hands together. "Awesome!" Hank laughed. "The fumes alone were enough to knock those uglies out cold!" Crank added.

Just then, the shuttle's crazy course smoothed out. Iggy beamed at the others. "You know what? I think I'm learning to fly this thing with one engine!"

"Oh!" Hank looked crestfallen. "Can't you go back to shaking us round and nearly crashing like before? That was the *best*!"

Teggs frowned. "You've had one knock on the head too many, Hank!"

The others all laughed, but Teggs had to force a smile. He felt strangely tense from tail to toes. Why? The danger was all over now . . .

Wasn't it?

On board the raptor shuttle, General Loki was rubbing his hands with glee. "Everything went exactly as planned!" he chuckled. "That idiot Teggs has no idea what we're really up to . . ."

"Excuse me, your horriblenessss," rasped one raptor warrior. "We have just detected T. rexes on Planet Sssixty."

"T. rexes?" Loki's single eye narrowed. "Why didn't you check before? Those brutes could have eaten the lot of us!" He swiped at the warrior, who yelped and fell to the floor. "Did that stupid stegosaurus get away safely?"

The raptor nodded quickly. "By the ssskin of his teeth."

"Good," said Loki. "I should hate for anything to happen to Captain Teggs." He chuckled nastily. "At least, not until he's done what we need him to do!"

Chapter Seven

MYSTERY

When it was learned that Captain Teggs had rescued the stegoceras athletes, there were celebrations all over the *Sauropod*.

The other athletes staged a big welcome back party for Hank and Crank.

Admiral Rosso sent special congratulations to the crew – "I knew you could do it!" he beamed.

The grateful organizers of the Great Dinosaur Games even offered Teggs and a guest two special seats in the royal paddock.

On the flight deck, Teggs was still glowing with pride. Soon he would be mingling with royalty! The kings and queens of every dinosaur race would be watching the games. This was the first time they had all gathered together in one place. It was a truly special occasion.

Then Teggs was jolted from his thoughts by a sudden clattering and whistling from the flock of flying reptiles around him.

"We're now in orbit around Olympus, Captain," Gipsy translated.

"I think the dimorphodon are as excited as we are!" She cleared her throat. "Er . . . have you decided who you're taking to the games?"

"Yes . . ." Teggs beamed at the stripy hadrosaur. "You! We'll take a shuttle down to the stadium with the other athletes in about one hour's time."

Gipsy grinned. "Yes, sir." But Teggs's good mood vanished when he saw Arx plodding over, shaking his horned head with worry.

"I've been studying all the data on our recent raptor adventures," said the triceratops. "And something's worrying me."

But before he could go on, the flight deck doors swept open to reveal Hank and Crank. Iggy stood proudly behind them.

"Welcome to the flight deck," said Teggs politely.

"We just realized, we never thanked you properly for paying the ransom to get us back," said Crank. "I bet it was a total fortune, right?"

Teggs and Arx swapped awkward looks.

"Er . . ." Teggs began, "*kind* of . . ."

"That's weird," said Gipsy suddenly. "I'm picking up a strange signal. It's interfering with our communicators."

"Find out where the signal's coming from," Teggs ordered, instantly alert.

"Wow, a captain's work is never done, huh?" grinned Hank. "Sorry to bug you when you're busy. We'll catch you later at the games."

"Yeah!" said Crank. "We're going to crack some serious skull down there, Captain — just for you!"

With that, the stegoceras athletes left the flight deck.

"Good lads," said Iggy quietly. "They'll do us herbivores proud!"

"That's funny, Captain," Gipsy reported. "The interference is clearing now. Just sort of fading away."

"Don't worry, Gipsy," said Teggs. "I'm sure it's probably nothing." He turned back to his first officer. "Now, what were you saying?"

"Listen, Captain," Arx said. "I checked the records for all recent raptor ransom demands. General Loki's demand for twenty gold pieces, a satellite monitor and some moss is actually the *lowest* ransom ever recorded."

"That monitor *was* a beauty, though," Iggy reminded them glumly.

Arx ignored him. "And remember when they got on board? They could've taken *all* the athletes. Why just take Hank and Crank?"

Teggs nodded slowly. "And if it was really money they were after, why not just steal it from the ship?"

"Why not indeed," said Arx. "Those raptors had us at their mercy – but they just gave up and flew away."

"What about those T. rexes on Planet Sixty?" Iggy argued. "I bet Loki knew they were down there. He was leading us into a trap."

"I don't think so," said Arx. "The raptors and T. rexes are fierce enemies."

Gipsy frowned. "Hang on, why did he pick Planet Sixty at all? It's light years away from the raptors' world."

"But very handy for us," said Arx, his horns glinting in the light. "It's on our way to the Dinosaur Games."

"That's crazy!" cried Iggy. "Why would the raptors want to make things easy for us?"

"There can only be one answer," said Teggs impressively.

Everyone looked at him.

Teggs swallowed nervously in the sudden spotlight. "Er . . . Because they *wanted* us to pick up the stegoceras athletes with no delays. They wanted us to get them to the games on time – whatever it took!"

Arx nodded. "I think you're right."

The dimorphodon flight crew clapped their leathery wings politely.

Iggy raised his voice over the applause. "Well, I don't know what they were planning, but security at the games is too tight for any funny business. You can't sneak a single stalk of celery in there without the security guards knowing about it." He sighed. "I should know, I've tried it!"

"Maybe so," said Teggs, turning to Gipsy. "But I think it's time we checked out the raptors' enclosure on Olympus. We've got plenty of questions. Now it's time to get the answers!"

Chapter Eight

RUMBLING THE RAPTORS

Teggs and Gipsy took a shuttle down to the planet's surface at top speed, while Arx and Iggy stayed on board the *Sauropod*.

"No sign of any raptor death ships in orbit," Arx's voice crackled from the communicator. "But the *Sauropod* is getting plenty of admiring looks from the other ships parked here!"

"So she should," grinned Teggs. "Keep an eye on things. Gipsy and I are going to head straight for the raptor enclosure."

"Good luck, sir," said Arx.

★

Teggs and Gipsy's royal passes got them swiftly through the crowds. No one dared to question where the two dinosaurs were going, and they soon reached the raptor enclosure.

This was where the raptors trained for the games. The rough floor was covered with bones and dark scraps. Teggs didn't want to examine them too closely. The whole place was sticky and shadowy, and it stank of raw meat.

"Quiet, isn't it?" Gipsy hissed.

"Too quiet," Teggs murmured uneasily. He hadn't expected to breeze straight to the heart of the raptors' den. They should have met *some* kind of obstacle by now!

Teggs crept on down the corridors as quietly as a seven-ton animal *can* creep. He thought longingly of the golden seats waiting for them in the royal paddock, glinting in the warm light from the planet's six suns. But a niggling feeling in his heavy bones told him that something bad was going to happen very soon – and that they didn't have long to stop it.

Teggs came to a sudden halt. He'd heard something up ahead – a distant buzzing sound. At first it sounded like a swarm of bees, but then he realized it was the sound of a mighty audience clapping and cheering over TV speakers.

Shuffling forwards, Teggs poked his head round the nearest open door, marked CENTRAL CONTROL. It was a large room with dark TV screens piled up along one wall. A raptor, wearing the peaked cap of a security guard, sat alone in a chair with its back to the screens. Its eyes were glued to a broadcast of the games' opening ceremony on a large monitor.

Teggs cleared his throat. "What do you think you're doing, you snivelling security guard?" he yelled.

The raptor leaped in the air like it had sat on a spike. "Just checking the ssstegocerasss were in position, sssir!" it hissed hurriedly.

"Oh yes?" Teggs frowned at the raptor. "In position for what?"

But the raptor had realized it was *not* explaining itself to its boss, but to some stupid herbivore! "You'll never know," it rasped. Eyes narrowed, it scuttled forwards and threw itself at Teggs's neck.

Luckily, Teggs ducked out of reach just in time. The raptor sailed out through the doorway and into the wall opposite. Gipsy jabbed the back of its neck with her big bill. The raptor collapsed, and she sat on it.

"Help!" it shrieked. "I can't move!"

"Answer the captain's questions and I'll sit somewhere else," said Gipsy sweetly.

"First question," said Teggs. "Where are all your raptor buddies?"

"Where it is sssafe," said the raptor smugly. Then it seemed to think it had said too much. "I mean — they are all out training, of courssse."

"Leaving only someone as dumb as you behind?" Teggs shook his head. "I don't think so. You raptors are up to something. You're working for General Loki, aren't you?"

"No way!" squealed the raptor. "I have never heard the name of our glorioussssly evil Commander of the Ssseven Fleetsss of Death, ruler of the meat mines of Raptosss, eater of edmontosssaurusss and devourer of . . . er . . . ever before in my life. Ever."

Teggs and Gipsy looked doubtfully at each other.

"Fibber," said Teggs.

The raptor gasped. "How did you know?"

Teggs smiled. "That satellite monitor you were watching. It's the one we gave you in return for Hank and Crank!"

"So what have you done to them?" said Gipsy. "Come on, talk –

or I'll jab you where it *really* hurts!"

"Don't, please!" yelped the guard. "I'm the only raptor left on the whole planet. Olympusss is doomed — thanks to your knuckle-headed friends!"

Teggs felt a shiver down his backbone. "What do you mean?"

"I mean," hissed the raptor nastily, "that when we kidnapped your athletesss, our doctors sssecretly placed a big bomb in their ssstupid skulls!"

"What?" gasped Gipsy.

The raptor nodded proudly. "When they bang their heads together hard enough, the bombs will go off — and the royal families of every dinosssaur race will be destroyed in a huge explosion!"

Teggs glared down at their prisoner. "You wouldn't dare! The whole quadrant would come after you for revenge!"

"But firssst there will be chaos," the

raptor hissed. "While every dinosssaur weeps in shock, our battle fleet shall attack their worlds."

Gipsy swallowed hard. "Taken by surprise, they won't stand a chance!"

The raptor laughed. "General Loki shall rule over half the galaxy!" It stared up at Teggs, eyes gleaming under the peak of its cap. "And it's all down to *you*, Captain! By bringing those head-butters here, *you've* helped it to happen!"

Chapter Nine

COUNTDOWN TO CARNAGE

"You're bluffing," Teggs decided. "Why should we believe you?"

"Captain," gasped Gipsy, her crest turning bright blue in alarm. "Remember that strange signal I picked up on the flight deck?"

Teggs nodded. "Sure."

"The signal started when Hank and Crank entered the flight deck, and stopped again when they left!" she said. "Don't you see? Those head bombs must've caused it!"

78

"We're in trouble," Teggs groaned.

The raptor chuckled. Gipsy jabbed her bill against the back of his head again and he fell silent.

Teggs turned up the volume on the satellite monitor. The commentator speaking was a brachiosaurus with a neck so long he could oversee the entire sprawling stadium.

"For the first time in fifty years, the royal families of every dinosaur race have been brought together," he said seriously. *"A spirit of friendly competition fills the air. Plant eaters and carnivores stand side by side in perfect peace. Of course, that big wire fence between them helps . . ."*

"How long before the games begin?" asked Gipsy.

"*It's almost three o'clock — almost time for the first event,*" said the commentator, as if he'd heard her question. "*That's the head-banging contest — also known as the Battle of the Butts . . .*"

"We've got so little time!" squealed Gipsy. "What can we do?"

"Hang on," said Teggs grimly. He began to nose about the raptors' security room. "I'll bet it's round here somewhere . . . aha!" he cried, shoving his head in a cupboard. "Just what's needed!"

"What have you found?" Gipsy asked breathlessly. "A way to defuse the bombs?"

"Nope — moss! It was part of the ransom, remember?" beamed Teggs. He pulled a massive green mouthful out of the cupboard. "I always think better on a full stomach." With that, he scoffed the lot and let out an enormous, satisfied belch. "Now, come on, Gipsy. No more dawdling – we've got a planet to save!"

Back on the *Sauropod*, high above the planet, Arx and Iggy were watching the countdown to the games on the scanner screen. Graceful pterodactyls soared through the air above the

stadium with cameras in their long jaws. They were beaming all the action live to a hundred worlds throughout the dinosaur empire.

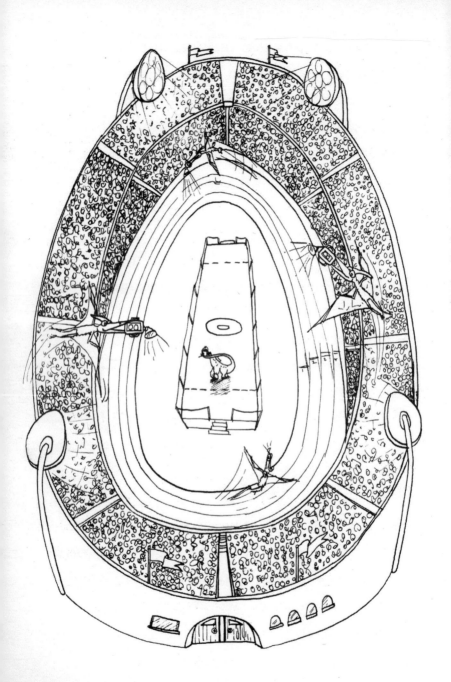

"Look," said Iggy, "Hank and Crank are first up to compete!"

"*And here are two true head-banging heroes,*" said the commentator, "*two plucky stegoceras with the hardest heads of any herbivore around . . . Hank and Crank!*"

The stadium, crammed with thousands of excited dinosaurs, shuddered with a giant roar of approval. Even the dimorphodon flight crew on the *Sauropod* stopped work for a while, watching attentively from perches all about the flight deck.

One pterodactyl zoomed in to show Hank and Crank circling each other on all fours, heads lowered . . .

"*Not long to go now, folks,*" came the commentator's voice. "*When the stadium clock strikes three times, the contest will begin. And I think we're in for some really explosive action today!*"

Teggs and Gipsy raced for the royal paddock. They knew they had to warn the kings and queens and cancel the contest.

They bundled down a long escalator lined with regal red carpet. Then, breathless, they approached the diamond-studded doors that led to the royal paddock.

Suddenly, five stubby-headed carnotaurus stewards appeared from nowhere, blocking the way. The stewards' tiny eyes glinted beneath the short, pointed horns on their eyelids.

"Can we help you?" asked one coldly.

"Even better," said another, "can we *eat* you?"

Teggs ignored him. "We need to get into the royal paddock," he panted.

"Oh yeah?" The first carnotaurus wrinkled its nostrils. "You don't look like royalty to me."

"We have special passes," said Teggs. "Gipsy?"

The colour drained from Gipsy's crest as she searched for them. "I've lost them!"

The stewards laughed, their tiny little forearms waggling with mirth. "You must think we hatched yesterday!" they cried.

Teggs glared at them and turned back to Gipsy. "You must have dropped them in the raptor enclosure. You know, when you sat on that security guard . . ."

He trailed off. The stewards had narrowed their eyes still further.

"What were a couple of royal herbivores doing inside a raptor enclosure?" asked the first, leaning forwards suspiciously. "Perhaps *you've* got something to do with the raptors not showing up to the games?"

Teggs groaned in despair. "We don't have time for this!"

Outside, the pterodactyls were still zooming through the air with their TV cameras. The commentator's voice echoed from the stadium: "*The tension mounts! In just a few moments the great clock will chime . . . and Hank and Crank will get butting!*"

"*Please!*" cried Gipsy. "We have to get out there and stop them!"

"Don't think so," snarled the second steward. "First, you have to get out of *here.*"

The five powerful predators advanced menacingly towards Teggs and Gipsy, drool dripping from their jaws . . .

Chapter Ten

DROPPING IN

"Sorry guys," said Teggs as he lashed
out at the nearest steward with his tail.
"But I think you'll thank me later!"
The carnotaurus was
knocked flying,
and the other
stewards leaped
back in surprise.
"Quick, Gipsy!"
he yelled. "Inside!"
   Together, they burst
into the royal paddock.
Close behind him came the
five stewards. Dinosaur kings and
queens gasped and shrieked as Teggs

and Gipsy pushed past them. They
spilled drinks, crushed crowns and sent
golden chairs scattering.

"Stop the contest!" Teggs yelled,
dodging the snapping jaws of the
nearest carnotaurus. "I'm a space
captain!"

"Look!" Gipsy cried.

She was staring in horror at an
enormous video screen.

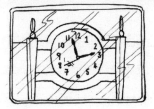

The pterodactyls had zoomed in on the great clock. It was edging ever closer towards three. They only had seconds to stop Hank and Crank from making the biggest bang in dinosaur history!

Suddenly, Teggs had a brilliant idea.

"The pterodactyls, Gipsy!" he shouted, almost trampling several queens as he dodged another steward. "The ones with the TV cameras! Maybe they can lift us out into the stadium!"

"It's worth a try, sir!" Gipsy nimbly hopped onto the back of a startled diplodocus. Quickly,

she whistled and clicked urgently at the flying reptiles high above them – just like she bossed about the dimorphodon on the *Sauropod*'s flight deck.

Teggs backed away from the angry carnotaurus stewards who had finally fenced him in. They advanced, closer and closer, jaws snapping, little hands twitching . . .

Suddenly, a dozen pterodactyls dived out of the sky. They dropped the TV cameras on the stewards' heads, and sent them sprawling.

Teggs grinned at Gipsy. "I'm glad you speak fluent pterosaur!"

"I told them what I'd do to them if they didn't help!" Gipsy winked. "I'm just glad they believed me!"

Gipsy clicked and whistled some

more. A moment later, Teggs felt the
armoured plates that ran down his
back being gripped and lifted by
twenty-four claws and twelve jaws.

The great clock chimed once. The
sound was almost drowned out by the
roar of the crowd.

"Quick!" yelled Teggs. Then his
stumpy legs were kicking the air as he
was lifted up, up into the sky.

The clock chimed twice.

Teggs gulped as he looked down. Gipsy was just a distant speck far below, but he thought he could hear her calling out. Wishing him luck.

"Good work, guys," he called to his flapping friends. He just hoped they spoke his language. "Now, see those orange nutters with the hard heads? Take me there!"

The clock chimed for the third and final time.

"Hurry!" Teggs bellowed.

As the crowd clapped and cheered, Hank and Crank ran out into the stadium.

"*Here we go, folks!*" the commentator cackled over the loudspeakers. "*These* hard-headed herbivores are ready for a bone-jarring skull-joust. I'm sure it'll be one we'll never forget!"

"Flap faster, fellas!" Teggs was almost directly above the athletes now . . .

Hank and Crank lowered their deadly heads. They were ready to charge . . .

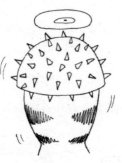

"Right!" roared Teggs. "Put me down! Quick!"

But to his horror, the pterodactyls did *exactly* as he asked – and simply let go of him.

With a yell of surprise, Teggs began to plummet from the sky like a miniature meteor.

Beneath him, in the stadium, the stegoceras began to charge forwards.

"Stop!" Teggs cried desperately. "You mustn't hit your heads!"

Perhaps Hank and Crank couldn't hear him.

Perhaps they just weren't listening.

They ran on, faster and faster, the gap between them closing, *closing* . . .

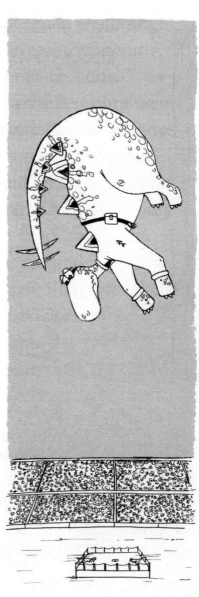

And then the skydiving Teggs finally hit the ground — right between Hank and Crank! He gasped as the air was bashed from his body.

The shocked crowd fell utterly silent.

Hank and Crank were running too fast to stop. They crashed into Teggs's belly, then bounced backwards.

"Ooof!" grunted Teggs, as he screwed his eyes tightly shut. He waited for the inevitable blast of the bombs.

But nothing happened.

As he gingerly opened his eyes again, Teggs saw a worried hadrosaur bounding over to join him.

"Captain!" Gipsy cried. "Are you all right?"

"This must be how the meteor felt when it hit the Earth!" groaned Teggs weakly.

Gipsy hugged him. "I thought it was all over when Hank and Crank ran into you!"

"Must be that moss I scoffed before setting off," said Teggs. "Made my stomach extra springy and squashy – so the bombs didn't go off!"

As the coos and chatter of the startled crowd began again, Teggs heard two weak groans on either side of him.

"Hank!" he gasped. "Crank! Are you guys OK?"

"I never read anything about a flying stegosaurus in the rules," Hank muttered. "But it's a cool idea!"

"Yeah, awesome!" Crank agreed feebly. "But can someone please get this tail off my face?"

Teggs was about to oblige when a massive, menacing shadow fell over the stadium. It was pointed and curved like an enormous claw, scratching out the sun.

The crowd fell silent.

And Teggs and Gipsy found

themselves staring up at the sinister
shape of a massive raptor death ship.

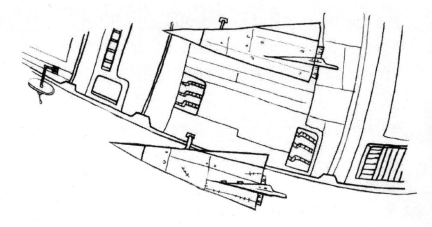

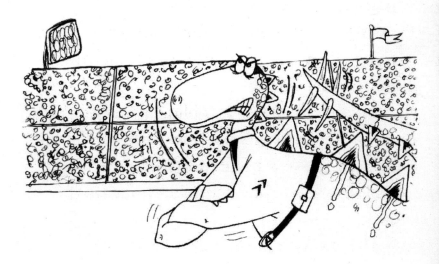

Chapter Eleven

THE FINAL CHALLENGE

"This is General Loki," an angry voice announced, booming out from the enormous spaceship. "I am Commander of the Seven Fleets of Death, ruler of the meat mines of Raptos, eater of— Well, you get the idea. Anyway – I bring an urgent message for Captain Teggs."

"Uh-oh," Teggs muttered. Gipsy tried to help him rise, but his legs were too bruised from the fall. He lay there helplessly, as if crushed into the ground by the weight of the ship's shadow.

"You've spoiled our evil plans, Captain," said Loki tetchily. "You've saved this entire, miserable planet from destruction."

A giant gasp went up from the crowd.

"Yes, I said *destruction*! If I had my way, you would all be space dust by now! But this pea-brained fool has spoiled all my plans—"

The crowd cheered and whooped.

"But you shall not enjoy your victory for long!" Loki added in his most sinister voice.

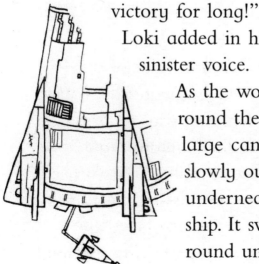

As the words echoed round the arena, a large cannon slid slowly out from underneath the raptor ship. It swivelled round until it was

aimed directly at Teggs. He and Gipsy
could only stare up at it helplessly.

But then another shadow fell. And
when Teggs saw what was casting it,
he grinned in amazement.

"This is the DSS *Sauropod*," Arx's voice
boomed out from the ship's speaker
system. "Perhaps you didn't hear,
General Loki? The raptors are a no-
show at this year's games – so get lost!"

With that, a volley of
laser fire tore loose
from the *Sauropod*.
As the red and
white lightning
burned and crackled
around the raptor
ship, the whole crowd
heard General Loki's howl of rage.

Then, with an ear-splitting sonic
boom, his death ship was sent spinning
away from the stadium. Soon, it had
vanished from view behind one of the
six scarlet suns glowing in the sky.

"We did it!" cried Gipsy, her crest
flushing bright red. "We saved the
planet!"

"*Ladies and gentlemen,*" announced the
bewildered commentator over the
speakers, "*it seems we owe a good deal
today to Captain Teggs − a truly amazing
astrosaur − and the crew of his fine ship, the
DSS* Sauropod!"

The crowd burst into thundering cheers and applause as the *Sauropod* flew slowly and gracefully off into orbit. Gipsy clapped too. Moments later, medics appeared. They swiftly tended to Teggs and the dazed athletes beside him.

As he was hefted away on a stretcher, Teggs smiled proudly up at the shrinking shape of his ship. He raised both his front legs in a dinosaur salute.

Some time later, Captain Teggs was back in his control pit, feasting on some of the finest ferns he had ever tasted. His legs felt much stronger, but he thought it best to take things easy for a while.

Beside him, Gipsy was busy reading aloud all the thank you messages they'd received.

"There's one here from Hank and Crank," she said happily. "The doctors have put their heads back to normal. But apparently they're really disappointed."

"Why?" wondered Teggs. "Because they couldn't take part in the games?"

"No," she chuckled. "Because they were hoping that exploding heads could become part of the sport!" She checked her read-out. "Hey, there's even a note from King Carnotaurus here. He says he's very sorry his stewards tried to eat you."

"No harm done," said Teggs briskly, turning to Arx. "Which I hope is more than can be said for General Loki?"

The triceratops smiled. "Iggy gave the lasers a power boost – enough to knock that raptor ship clear out of orbit! There's no telling where they'll end up!"

"Actually," said Iggy slyly, "there *is*." He gave Teggs a wicked grin. "I took a look with the long-range scanners, Captain. And guess what! Loki's ship will be forced to land for repairs somewhere around here . . ."

Iggy turned on the scanner with his stiff little tail and soon Teggs was staring at the green disc of a very familiar planet.

"Planet Sixty!" he beamed. "Really?"

"Serves them right," laughed Arx. "I wonder if that group of T. rexes is still there?"

Gipsy grinned. "They'll certainly keep Loki busy for a while!"

"And what about us?" asked Iggy. "I like to be kept busy too!"

"Take it easy while you can," came a booming voice. Everyone looked up to see a crusty old barosaurus on the scanner screen.

"Admiral Rosso!" gasped Gipsy.

"That's right!" he beamed. "I just

wanted to congratulate you all on a job well done."

"Thank you, sir," said Teggs.

"Thank *you*," the admiral nodded. "You've come through your first mission with flying colours."

"And flying stegosaurs, too!" whispered Gipsy, nudging Teggs in the ribs.

"We couldn't have done it without the *Sauropod*, sir," Teggs told him, helping himself to an extra-big mouthful of delicious ferns. "She's a fine ship."

"And she has a fine crew," said the admiral with a smile. "And you know what? I have a hunch that somewhere out there, a new adventure's waiting . . . just around the corner."

Admiral Rosso's face faded from the screen.

Now the scanner showed the view outside the ship: the endless sparkle and

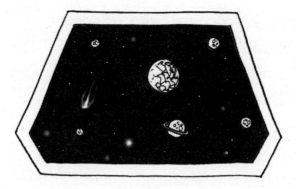

darkness of deep space. Teggs stared at it dreamily. He couldn't wait to explore it all.

"Well," he said. "I think we should get going."

Arx raised a bony eyebrow. "Where to, Captain?"

"You heard the admiral – just around the corner!" Teggs winked at him. "Don't you know it's rude to leave an adventure waiting?"

THE END

TALKING DINOSAUR!

STEGOSAURUS –
STEG-oh-SORE-us

PTEROSAUR –
TEH-roh-sore

BAROSAURUS –
bar-oh-SORE-us

HADROSAUR –
HAD-roh-sore

TRICERATOPS –
try-SERRA-tops

IGUANODON –
ig-WA-noh-don

ORNITHOMIMOSAUR –
OR-ni-thoh-MEE-moh-sore

DIMORPHODON –
die-MORF-oh-don

VELOCIRAPTOR –
vel-ossi-RAP-tor

ANKYLOSAURUS –
an-KI-loh-SORE-us

SALTASAURUS –
sal-te-SORE-us

MAIASAURA –
MY-ah-SORE-ah

STEGOCERAS –
ste-GOS-er-as

EDMONTOSAURUS –
ed-MON-toh-SORE-us

DIPLODOCUS –
di-PLOH-do-kus

TYRANNOSAURUS –
tie-RAN-oh-SORE-us

CARNOTAURUS –
kar-noh-TOR-us

BRACHIOSAURUS –
brak-ee-oh-SORE-us

PTERODACTYL –
teh-roh-DACT-il

THE SEAS OF DOOM

By Steve Cole

Illustrated by
Woody Fox

For Annie and James

Chapter One

A SOGGY MISSION

In orbit high above the planet Aqua Minor, Captain Teggs Stegosaur was waiting to start his next adventure.

He was waiting *very* impatiently.

"Admiral Rosso had better call us soon," Teggs grumbled, chomping on the delicious moss that covered his control pit. "I can't wait to find out why we've been sent to the soggiest planet in the Jurassic Quadrant!"

"I'm sure it won't be much longer, Captain," said Arx Orano, the triceratops beside him.

Sitting around twiddling his thumbs wasn't easy for the young, daredevil stegosaurus. He didn't have any thumbs, for a start.

Teggs commanded the DSS *Sauropod*, the finest ship in the Dinosaur Space Service. He and his crew were all highly trained astrosaurs. They flew through space helping plant-eaters in peril – wherever the planet, whatever the risk.

But why had the *Sauropod* been sent to a world full of *fish*?

"Maybe Admiral Rosso thinks we need a holiday by the seaside," said Iggy Tooth, the *Sauropod*'s Chief Engineer. A brave iguanodon, he was

clever with machines and fiercely loyal
to his captain. "I don't really like the
seaside. I'm not keen on fish. I met a
fish with no eyes, once."

"That would make it a *fsh*. Get it?"
called Gipsy Saurine from her seat.
Gipsy was a duck-billed hadrosaur with
scaly, stripy skin. She handled the ship's
communications and much more
besides. "Anyway, there *is* no seaside on
Aqua Minor. Only sea!"

"Calling Captain Teggs . . ." The gruff voice of Admiral Rosso, the crusty old barosaurus in charge of the Dinosaur Space Service, suddenly crackled from the *Sauropod*'s speakers. "Captain Teggs, can you hear me?"

"At last!" spluttered Teggs through a mouthful of moss. He rose up from the control pit – eight metres long from tail to beak, with jagged bony plates running down his orange-brown back.

Gipsy trotted over to Teggs. "Shall I put the admiral on the scanner screen, Captain?" she asked.

"Yes please," said Teggs.

Gipsy whistled the order through her snout to the dimorphodon. These plucky pterosaurs were the *Sauropod*'s flight crew, and they loved to be bossed about.

The team leader flapped down and pecked the scanner control happily

120

with his beak. A moment later, Admiral
Rosso's wrinkled face appeared.

"Ah, there you are, Teggs," said the
old barosaurus. "Sorry to keep you
waiting, but running an entire space
fleet keeps me busy. And when you get
to my age . . ."

Teggs saluted. "What's up, sir?"

"It's what's *down* that's worrying us,"
said Admiral Rosso. "Down below!"

Arx and Gipsy swapped puzzled looks.
But Teggs just smiled at the thought of
a brand new adventure beginning at
last.

"Something very big and very dangerous is swimming about in the seas of Aqua Minor," the admiral went on. "The cryptoclidus who go fishing there are getting very worried."

Teggs frowned. "Crypto-who?"

"A race of sea reptiles from the planet Cryptos," Arx explained. "They have run out of food in their own world, so now they fish the waters of Aqua Minor for squid and shellfish. Then they send it by rocket to the folk back home."

"Very good, Arx," smiled Admiral Rosso. "Teggs, you have a first-rate first officer there!"

"He's the best," Teggs agreed. "So, what's been happening on Aqua Minor?"

"Five undersea fish factories have been

wrecked, along with several submarines." Admiral Rosso sighed. "But no one knows who's doing it – or why!"

Teggs nodded. "And you want us to find out."

"That's right," said Admiral Rosso. "The cryptoclidus may not be vegetarians, but they are still our friends and neighbours in space. They've asked us for help in solving this mystery."

"So what are we waiting for?" asked Teggs. "Let's get to Aqua Minor and see what we can find!"

Once Admiral Rosso had given them a map and some orders, Teggs, Gipsy and Arx went to the shuttle bay. The air was smoky and thick with the smell of the burning dung that fuelled the engines. Iggy Tooth was waiting for them by the shuttle.

"The engines are all fired up, Captain!" said the stocky iguanodon. "We're ready to go!"

Once they were safely strapped in, the shuttle blasted off. Soon they were soaring through the brilliant blue skies of Aqua Minor.

"Wow!" said Teggs, peering through the window. "What a view. There's so much sea to see!"

Below them, the ocean stretched out endlessly to the horizon. Enormous spaceships floated above the waves,

trailing fishing nets behind them. Teggs watched one spaceship rise higher than the rest. Its net was bulging with shimmering, silvery shellfish that sparkled in the bright sunlight.

"No wonder the cryptoclidus need our help," said Arx. "This is a very big ocean for something nasty to hide in."

"Where are we going to park the shuttle?" asked Iggy.

"On one of their floating factories," said Gipsy, checking her wrist tracker. "It's not far from here."

"It was the first place to be attacked, a month ago," said Teggs. "We'll take a look and search for clues."

Soon the floating factory came into sight. It looked like a large square of shiny metal, covered in long huts. In the middle of the square, a small, grey shape started waving at them.

"Who's that?" asked Iggy, as they came in to land.

"That must be Commander Cripes," said Arx. "He'll be showing us around."

The shuttle landed safely, and its doors slid open. A strong smell of shellfish filled the air.

As the astrosaurs stepped outside, Cripes came waddling up to greet them. Like all cryptoclidus, he looked like a cross between a seal and the Loch Ness monster. He had a long neck and four flat flippers, and his belly dragged on the ground as he moved. A broad-brimmed hat was perched on his head, and a shiny cape kept the sun off his long, smooth back.

"Welcome to Aqua Minor, guys," said Cripes. "Admiral Rosso said you were on your way. Glad you could make it!"

"Thanks," said Teggs. "This is Arx, and this is Iggy."

Cripes smiled. "And this cute little hadrosaur just *has* to be Gipsy." He took her hoof in his flipper and kissed it. "Now, let me show you around. This factory stretches down almost to the sea bed . . ."

Cripes led them into a hut and then into a large lift. It took them down deep under the water. When it finally stopped, Teggs led the way out into a large, crumbling workplace. The machines and conveyor belts stood silent. The walls were cracked. The floor was flooded with smelly, oily water.

"Hard to believe that this place was brand new six weeks ago, isn't it?" sighed Cripes. "Just two weeks after opening, *this* happened."

Teggs stared around. "Something has torn the whole place apart!"

"And this was just the first attack,"

Cripes reminded him. "In the last month there have been lots more. Every new factory we build in this area gets wrecked!"

"What are they used for anyway?" asked Gipsy.

"The floating factories prepare the fish we catch before we send it back home to feed our people," Cripes explained. "On the bottom levels, we suck in thousands of ammonites and belemnites from the pens on the sea bed. We  take off the shells and rinse them clean. And then a submarine delivers them here for packaging."

"We're under the sea, aren't we?" asked Iggy. "So how come this place isn't full of water?"

"We cryptoclidus live on land as well as in the sea," Cripes reminded him.

"The food is easier to pack when it's not floating around all over the place!"

Arx plodded over to a wall and prodded a button with his longest horn. Everyone jumped as the machines sparked into life. The conveyor belt jerked forwards. Metal scoops swung down from the wonky ceiling.

"Cool – the machines still work!" shouted Teggs over all the noise. "What do they do?"

"The shellfish plop out of this pipe here onto the conveyor belt," Cripes explained over the din. "Then they're wrapped up in the wrapping machine

and sent upstairs to the spaceships. But nothing has come through that pipe for weeks and in the meantime, the people back home are going hungry."

Teggs felt sad watching the ruined machines clanking away with no purpose. But before he could turn them off, he felt the ground shake beneath his feet.

"That's not the builders starting work on the repairs already, is it?" asked Gipsy nervously.

Suddenly, the whole factory rocked as if a giant had kicked it. The astrosaurs were knocked off their feet. The cracks in the walls widened. The floor broke open beneath them, and sea water began rushing in.

"Never mind the builders!" cried Teggs over the din of the machines and the churning water. "I think the thing that attacked this place before has come back to finish it off!"

Chapter Two

THE SINISTER SHADOW

"Quick, you guys!" yelled Commander Cripes. "Back to the lift!"

Iggy and Gipsy didn't need telling twice. They quickly splashed over to the lift. Teggs and Arx began to follow. But before they could reach the others, the floor before them crumbled away into the water.

"We're cut off!" cried Arx.

"Iggy! Gipsy!" shouted Teggs. "Get out of here now, while you can!"

"But we can't leave you!" called Gipsy. "You'll drown!"

"That's an order!" Teggs bellowed.

Iggy sadly saluted him, and Cripes

pressed a button. The lift clanked slowly upwards.

"We'll get help!" Gipsy called. Then they were gone.

Arx yelped as a large chunk of falling ceiling nearly squashed him. "Come away from the edge, Captain!" he shouted. "If you fall down there you'll never get out again!"

"Wait!" Teggs called, rooted to the spot. "Look! Something's moving down there!"

Arx edged closer. Sure enough he saw a dark shadow in the oily water. It looked like the shadow of something very big and very, very dangerous.

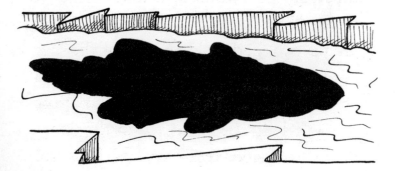

"If only we could get a closer look at it," said Teggs.

"Captain," Arx gasped. "If the water level keeps rising, *it* might swim up here to get a closer look at *us*!"

Together they backed away from the edge. The freezing cold water was now up to their chins.

"This looks like the end," sighed Arx.

"We'll find a way out," said Teggs bravely. He tried to think, but it wasn't easy with the noise of the clanking machines all around him.

Then he had a brainwave.

"The machines!" he cried. "If we can climb up onto the machines, we'll be higher up. The water will take longer to reach us!"

Teggs grabbed hold of one of the dangling scoops with his beak. He used it to haul himself up onto the clanking conveyor belt. Arx tried to do the same, but he struggled. Teggs wrapped his tail round the triceratops's head frill and helped him up.

"Now the water only comes up to our toes!" beamed Teggs.

"But we're heading for the wrapping machine!" cried Arx. "It'll squash us into a parcel!"

"No, it won't," said Teggs, smashing his big, bony tail into the machine. It exploded in a cloud of sparks. "I think it's out of order!" he grinned.

As the sparks died away, the machines suddenly stopped. The room fell eerily quiet. The only sound was the swoosh of the sea water beneath them.

"I guess I caused a short circuit," said Teggs.

"At least we can hear ourselves think now," said Arx. He paused. "Er, Captain . . . can you hear what I hear?"

Teggs listened. "I can't hear anything."

"Exactly!" said Arx. "Whatever was attacking us, it seems to have given up!"

Teggs peered over the edge of the conveyor belt. There was no sign of the dark shadow beneath the sea. "I think you're right," he whispered.

But then something large and white came whizzing up through the water.

"Look out!" yelled Teggs.

The big white thing burst out of the sea below them with a massive splash. A huge wave of water crashed over Teggs and Arx, blinding them both.

"It's a sea monster!" shouted Arx, blinking furiously.

"Get behind me, Arx!" cried Teggs, his eyes stinging. "I'll fight it off!"

"Actually," said a familiar voice, "I only wanted to give you a lift!"

Teggs grinned with delight as he blinked away the last of the saltwater. "Iggy!" he cheered.

The big white thing was only the shuttle. Now it bobbed about on the water in front of them, like a giant rubber duck in a very big bath. Iggy stood in the doorway.

Gipsy leaned out behind him and waved. "We thought this might be a good time to see if the shuttle works underwater."

"Luckily it does!" added Cripes, peering over Gipsy's shoulder. "At least for short trips!"

"Good work, guys," said Teggs as he leaped aboard. "Come on, there's no time to lose. We just saw something very big swimming about down here. Let's try to follow it!"

"That's risky, Captain," said Arx. "That thing must be big enough to swallow the shuttle in one gulp!"

"It's a risk we'll have to take," Teggs told him.

Once Arx had scrambled into the shuttle, they set off. Like a submarine, the little ship ducked under the waves and hummed quietly through the clear

green water. But all they saw were shoals of tiny fish swimming past them. There was no sign of the mysterious dark thing.

"How could it just vanish?" wondered Teggs.

Suddenly a warning light came on in the shuttle.

"Sea water is getting into the engine pipes," said Iggy.

"OK, Iggy," sighed Teggs. "Better head back to the surface, fast!"

"Aye-aye, Captain," said Iggy.

He steered the shuttle sharply upwards. A few seconds later, it burst from the sea like a great white whale. The warning light went out, and everyone breathed a sigh of relief.

Teggs turned to Cripes. "Is there somewhere we can go to plan our next move?"

"The nearest base is Sea Station One, fifty miles north of here. It's where the fishing teams live while they're staying on Aqua Minor."

"Will the shuttle get us that far?" asked Arx.

"Just about," said Iggy. "We don't have enough power to fly, but we can chug along the surface like a motorboat!"

"Good," said Teggs with a grin. "I just hope there'll be some food about. I'm *starving*!"

Chapter Three

DEEP DOWN DANGER

"Wow!" said Gipsy as the shuttle sailed into sight of Sea Station One. It was like a cross between a grand hotel, a beautiful harbour and a busy spaceport. Some cryptoclidus were splashing about in enormous pools of salty water. Others sat in cafés eating buckets of fish.

In the distance, rockets blasted off from the floating factories, filled with food to take home to Cryptos. And as Gipsy followed her friends off the shuttle, a large oily tugboat sailed in to the sea station, filled with gangs of chattering cryptoclidus.

She turned to Cripes. "What do you need old-fashioned boats for? I thought you had spaceships to pull your nets?"

"The tugboats ferry our workers to and from the floating factories," Cripes explained. "Few of us dare to swim in the sea at the moment."

"Well, we'll have to *sea* what we can do about that," Teggs chuckled.

"Have you marked where the monster attacks took place?" asked Arx.

Cripes took out a map of Aqua Minor from his raincoat and Gipsy helped him unfold it. "X marks the spot," he said. "*Several* spots."

"So all five attacks took place in the south of the planet," noted Arx.

"That's right," said Cripes. "All our other floating factories are in the north. We've been trying to build new ones in the south to meet the demand for shellfish back home . . ."

"But every single one has been destroyed," growled Iggy.

"It looks like someone – or something – is fed up with you fishing here," said Gipsy.

"And it's our job to find out who," said Teggs bravely. "Once we've had a quick snack . . ."

"Of course." Cripes led them to the nearest café and slapped his flippers together. A waiter paddled straight over with a massive plate of sticky, slimy seaweed.

Teggs took a cautious nibble. It tasted like a wet, salty dishcloth.

"Delicious," gasped Teggs weakly. "But perhaps I'll skip the snack. I should start searching the sea."

"I'll come with you," said Gipsy.

"You know it's risky," Cripes warned them.

"Of course," beamed Teggs. "But if we're to help you, we need to find out more."

"I wish I could let you guys take a sub," said Cripes. "But we don't have any left. We tried looking for the monster in them. But the subs are so noisy, I guess the monster heard us coming a mile away. It chewed them all up!"

Gipsy looked worried. "Did the pilots get out?"

"Only just," said Cripes. "They were lucky to escape with their lives! But by the time they'd wriggled out of the wrecks, there was no sign of the monster at all." He clicked his tongue. "Oh, well. Maybe you'll have more luck in the diving bell."

"What's a diving bell?" asked Teggs.

"It's like a big metal case with a window in the side," Arx explained. "It'll take you underwater!"

"We take you out to sea," said Cripes. "Then we lower you down into the water on a chain so you can take a good look about."

"How will we breathe?" asked Teggs.

"It's completely airtight," Cripes assured him. "But there's also deep-sea diving gear on board in case of emergencies."

"What if we get into trouble?" asked Gipsy.

"Just press the help button," said Cripes. "We'll have you back out again in no time!"

"Fair enough," said Teggs. "Meanwhile, I'd like Arx to check over those chewed-up subs for clues."

"No problem," Cripes told him. "They're all piled up in a storeroom downstairs."

"Can I see some wreckage from that floating factory, too?" asked Arx.

"We'll pick some up for you." Cripes

rose and adjusted his hat. "Well, if you guys are ready . . ."

"We sure are!" Teggs jumped to his feet. "Let's get going!"

The shuttle's engines were still soggy, so Cripes took them out in one of the tugboats to the wreck of the floating factory. Teggs was wearing his battle armour, and Gipsy had slipped on her combat suit.

"I've never tried using my electro-tail underwater," said Teggs thoughtfully.

"Arx said our armour would work wherever we were," said Gipsy. "And if we do meet any monsters down there, I'm glad about that!"

Once they had reached the wreck, Teggs and Gipsy squeezed inside the orange diving bell.

There was just room for the two of them and the diving gear.

Cripes waved at them through the window. "On top of the bell is a special camera," he said. "It can see through murky water. So if you *do* find a nasty sea monster down there, we should get a good picture of it."

"We'll ask it to say cheese," joked Teggs.

"Good luck, guys," said Cripes. Iggy pressed a big green button, and Gipsy squealed as the bell was heaved up over the side of the ship on heavy chains.

"This is better than a funfair ride!" Teggs declared. He looked out through the large window in the side of the bell. On the ship's deck, Iggy stood beside Cripes. He gave a small, worried wave to his captain.

Slowly, the diving bell was lowered into the water. Teggs and Gipsy were soon staring out at an undersea world. Curious fish swam up to see them.

Deeper and deeper they went. A friendly squid blinked at them as it drifted by. A weird, spindly fish spiralled lazily past.

The bell came to rest on the sea bed with a soft bump. The water through the window was cloudy and dark. Nothing moved. Nothing stirred at all.

Gipsy felt a shiver go through her. "I hope this thing doesn't leak," she said.

Teggs nodded. "Let's put on the diving gear, just in case."

They helped each other strap oxygen tanks to their necks. Then they put on special diving helmets.

"Now we'll be ready for anything," beamed Teggs.

But neither of them was ready for what happened next.

Wham!

The diving bell shook with an enormous blow.

"What was that?" gasped Gipsy.

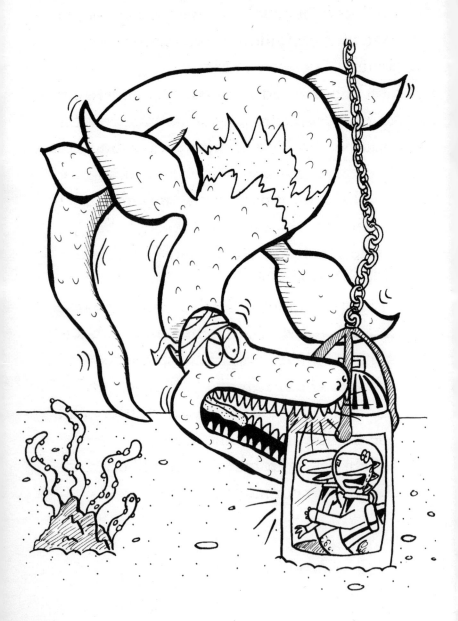

"I don't know!" said Teggs. He peered out of the window – and wished he hadn't.

A massive sea monster was staring in at them with huge, yellow eyes. Its skin was a deep blotchy blue and white. Its head was the size of a sofa, and the top of it was wrapped in a tatty bandage. It was easily three times as long as Teggs, and its flippers were the size of small trees.

The sea monster smiled, revealing a long row of terrifying teeth. Then it attacked the diving bell. Its teeth tore through the metal like it was wet cardboard. Sea water flooded in through the gaping hole in the wall.

"Hit the help button, Gipsy!" cried Teggs. "It's coming to get us!"

Chapter Four

THE MONSTER

Up on the tugboat, the chain holding the diving bell was swinging about like a piece of string in a gale.

"Something's wrong!" gasped Iggy. "Quick! Bring up the bell!"

Cripes hit a yellow button on his control panel. The chain clanked and heaved – but the diving bell wouldn't rise.

"It's jammed!" cried Cripes. "Something's got hold of it!"

"I'll boost the power," said Iggy. He fiddled with some wires beneath the control panel. "Try it now!"

Cripes pressed the button again. This time, the bell began to move from the sea bed.

He beamed at Iggy. "You did it!"

Iggy and Cripes waited tensely. Finally, the diving bell emerged from the foaming waters.

Or what was left of it.

The bell had been mangled and squashed. Half of it was missing altogether. But most worrying of all, it was completely empty.

"Teggs and Gipsy . . ." breathed Iggy. "They've gone!"

"But so has their diving gear," said Cripes, peering inside. "Maybe they got away."

"If they did, they're still too heavy to swim up from the bottom of the sea!" wailed Iggy. "We have to find them – fast!"

Cripes clapped his flippers. Two

cryptoclidus sailors in white caps and overalls slithered up to him.

"We need to get a search party down there, guys," said Cripes. "Ten of your fastest swimmers, right now!"

The two sailors nodded. "Straight away, sir," they cried, and then dashed off.

Iggy sighed, wishing the shuttle worked better underwater so he could look for himself. "How long can Teggs and Gipsy stay down there?"

"Let me see . . ." Cripes counted on his flippers. "They should have enough air to last three hours. After that . . ."

Iggy looked very glum. "I suppose I'd better tell Arx the bad news," he said.

"We won't just tell him," said Cripes gravely. "We'll *show* him." He pointed a flipper at the mangled diving bell. "The undersea camera is still there. We'll take it back with us and see just what happened."

"Well, what are we waiting for?" cried Iggy. "Let's get going!"

★

Iggy and Cripes found Arx busy
working in the storeroom full of broken
subs and wreckage from the floating
factory. When the triceratops heard
what had happened to the diving bell,
his horns seemed to droop.

"Don't worry, Arx. The search party
will find them soon and carry them
safely back up to the surface," said Iggy
stoutly. "Right, Cripes?"

"I hope so," said Cripes. He pulled out
the camera from under his cape. "In the

meantime, these pictures should be ready. Let's see what happened down there."

Arx and Iggy gathered round him as he pulled the back off the camera. Inside was a set of pictures, bone-dry and crystal-clear. Always impressed by a good invention, Arx was about to compliment Cripes on his clever camera. But he lost his voice when he saw what the pictures showed.

One showed the massive blue and white monster swimming up to the bell.

Another showed its enormous flippers and terrible tail.

"Look at the size of that thing!" gasped Cripes. "It's as big as a battleship!"

He quickly
sorted through
more of the
pictures. They
showed the

monster grinning wildly, and then
tearing through the metal of the diving
bell. It seemed dead set on getting to
Gipsy and Teggs.

"It should pick on someone its own
size," said Iggy fiercely.

Cripes gulped. "There *is* no one else
its own size!"

The second-to-
last picture showed
Teggs and Gipsy
standing on the sea
bed in their diving
gear. They were
looking up at the fearsome creature.

"No!" groaned Iggy. "I don't want to
see what happened next!"

"I'm afraid we must," said Arx quietly.

But the last of the pictures showed only the empty sea bed.

"Where did they go?" demanded Iggy. "It's like they just vanished!"

"At least there's no sign that they were hurt," said Cripes.

Arx nodded slowly. "And at least now we know that a *liopleurodon* is hiding down there in the deeps," he said.

Iggy frowned. "A what?"

"Back on Earth it was the biggest, nastiest killing machine in the water!" Arx went on. "You're looking at one hundred tons of swimming death!"

"It . . . it can't be true!" stammered Cripes. "The liopleurodon rule those huge water worlds on the edge of the Jurassic Quadrant. No one has visited them for hundreds of years – they wouldn't dare!"

"Maybe not," said Arx darkly. "But it seems the liopleurodon have dared to visit Aqua Minor!"

"If it *is* just a visit," growled Iggy. "This could be the start of an invasion!"

"But I don't understand!" Cripes started shivering. "A liopleurodon ship couldn't land here without us knowing about it. And we've been fishing on Aqua Minor for five years without any trouble!"

"Oh, come on! Wakey-wakey!" cried Iggy. He waved the pictures in Cripes's face. "What more proof do you need? There's a liopleurodon out there! It's  been smashing up your factories, eating your subs and scaring everyone silly – and now it's got Teggs and Gipsy!"

Chapter Five

A STRANGE FRIEND

Back at the bottom of the sea, Teggs
and Gipsy were facing up to the
massive monster with the bandaged
head.

Once the liopleurodon had ripped apart the diving bell, he floated in the water, watching them closely. Teggs had pulled his scariest face and swished his armoured tail through the water. Gipsy was ready to jab their attacker on the nose if he came any closer.

But they were both surprised to find that the liopleurodon had no plans to eat them alive.

In fact, he was very polite.

"Right then!" he said brightly. Bubbles streamed out of his mouth as he spoke. "I've got you out of that horrible prison. Now you can come home with me!"

Teggs and Gipsy stared at each other in amazement through their diving helmets.

"What do you mean?" Gipsy cried. "That wasn't a prison!"

"Of course it was!" said the liopleurodon. "You were both squished up inside! Trapped by those flipper-flappers! Locked up and hanging from a chain! But now you're free!"

The sea monster smiled happily. He was clearly very pleased with himself.

Teggs turned to Gipsy. "What's a flipper-flapper?"

167

"It must be his word for the cryptoclidus," Gipsy whispered back.

Teggs cleared his throat. "Well, thanks for trying to help," he said. But without that, er, *prison* as you call it, we can't get back up to the surface!"

"Why would you want to do that?" asked the liopleurodon, baffled. "The flipper-flappers would only lock you up again. No, no, the likes of us should stick together."

"What do you mean?" asked Gipsy.

"Well, *you're* not flipper-flappers. *I'm* not a flipper-flapper. But everyone else on the planet *is!*"

Teggs looked at him thoughtfully. "Who are you?"

"I think my name must be Mira," said the liopleurodon. "That's what is written

on my outfit,
anyway!" He
spun round to
show them a
torn scrap of
blue uniform
that clung to
his middle. The
word MIRA was
spelled out in gold thread.

"You mean you don't even know your
own *name*?" asked Teggs.

"Nope!" said Mira cheerfully. "I must
have been bumped on the head at some
point. I'm sure I'm not just wearing this
bandage because it looks pretty."

"That's for sure," murmured Gipsy.

"Anyway," said Mira. "Now that I've
set you free, you must help me find my
spaceship! I'm sure I parked it round
here somewhere, but that was a long,
long time ago." He gave a sad little
sigh. "I've been searching ever since."

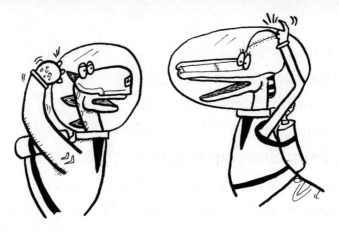

"You parked a spaceship under the sea?" Teggs turned to Gipsy. "Bump on the head or not, this so-called sea monster is a nut!" he hissed.

Gipsy nodded. "But he's a very big, very dangerous nut with *extremely* big teeth!" she pointed out. "We'd better not upset him."

"Well?" asked Mira. His gleaming eyes narrowed a little. "*Are* you going to help me?"

Teggs gulped. "Umm . . . Yes."

"Hurrah!" cried Mira, brightening again. "I know it's round here somewhere. We're bound to find it soon. Follow me!"

Gipsy cleared her throat. "Actually, I think we should stay here—"

"Follow me!" Mira yelled crossly, cutting her off. "My cave is this way."

Teggs and Gipsy couldn't move very fast underwater. They shivered in the awful cold. Their heavy bodies ached as they trudged over the thick dark sand.

"We have to get back to the surface," muttered Gipsy. "We don't have enough air to stay down here for long."

"I know," said Teggs. "But how?"

Mira kept swimming round them in a big circle. "Keep up!" he yelled. "I can't wait to show you my cave! It's ever so cosy, and you'll love the colours! I've chosen brown rock, with bits of darker brown rock and just a hint of very, *very* brown rock . . ."

"This Mira is as batty as a belemnite," said Teggs quietly. "But he seems friendly enough."

Gipsy nodded. "So why has he been attacking factories and submarines?"

"What?" asked Mira, zooming up behind them. "Me? Attack factories and submarines? Why would I do that?"

"You tell us," said Teggs bravely. "That's what you've been doing, isn't it?"

"Don't be so silly," said Mira, floating upside down and going cross-eyed. "I've never attacked a factory in my life! I stay well away from those flipper-flappers with their big nets. I don't want to get caught!"

Gipsy turned back to Teggs. "Do you believe him?" she whispered.

"I don't know," said Teggs. "But why would he bother to lie? He could eat us alive in a couple of bites!"

"Stop chatting and get a move on!" nagged Mira. "Honestly, dinner will be ruined!"

Teggs perked up. "Dinner?"

"Yes!" cried Mira, waggling his flippers. "Din-dins! Come on! Come and get it!"

"Brilliant!" Teggs quickened his step. He was still starving.

"But *Captain* . . ." Gipsy tapped his diving helmet with her hoof. "How are you going to eat through *that* thing?"

"Arrgh!" Teggs groaned. "I'm going as nutty as Mira!"

But when they finally reached the liopleurodon's lair, Teggs found he was glad to miss Mira's meal. It was floating all about them in the cold, dark water – tons and tons of raw, rotten squid!

"Come on, chaps! Dig in!" Mira beamed. "Took me ages to catch this lot!"

"Oh." Gipsy swapped an awkward look with Teggs. "Sorry, Mira, but we're, er, not really hungry."

"Not hungry?" Mira looked hurt. "But . . . I wanted to celebrate meeting you. I've been very lonely down here on my own, you know." Mira opened his giant jaws and guzzled down fifty squid in a single gulp. "So take those glass hats off your heads and tuck in!"

"We can't!" said Teggs.

"Of course you can," said Mira briskly. "No need to be shy."

"But we can't breathe in water like you do," Teggs protested.

Mira folded his fins firmly. "Take them *off.*"

"If we do, we'll drown!" cried Gipsy.

"Drown? Don't be so silly!" said Mira crossly. "Only the flipper-flappers breathe air. *We* live in the sea!" He came closer. "And if you won't take off those silly glass bubbles yourselves . . . I'll take them off for you!"

Mira's mouth swung open, revealing rows of lethal teeth, as he lunged towards them . . .

Chapter Six

HIDE AND SEEK

Teggs and Gipsy dived out of the way –
just in time. Mira's razor-sharp teeth
scratched the side of Gipsy's glass helmet.

"Let me wear it, *please!*" she begged Mira.

"What a lot of fuss you're making!"
Mira tutted. "The silly
thing doesn't
even suit you!"
He opened
his mouth
again to pluck
off Gipsy's
diving helmet.
This time, he
couldn't miss . . .

Teggs flexed his armoured tail, ready
to whack Mira right on the flipper. But
as his tail swung back it struck some
rotten squid floating in the water. The
power in his armour sparked through
them – and made them glow a spooky
electric blue!

Mira moaned in horror. "Ghosts!" he cried. "My breakfast has come back to haunt me!" A cloud of bubbles burst from his behind. "Aaaaagh!"

With that, the terrified giant sped from the cave.

"What a brilliant plan, Captain!" said Gipsy admiringly. "But how did you know that using your electro-tail underwater would light up anything it touched?"

Teggs stared at the glowing squid. He was almost as surprised as Mira. Then he grinned. "You know me, Gipsy," he said. "I may have a brain the size of an acorn, but I've always been a bright spark! Come on, let's get out of here before Mira comes back!"

They quickly left the cave. The water was dark and gloomy as they tried to retrace their steps across the sea bed. But it was hard to tell which way they should go. At the bottom of the sea, everything looked the same – dark and spooky.

Soon, Teggs and Gipsy realized they were totally lost.

"We're running out of air, Captain," said Gipsy.

"Someone will find us soon!" Teggs said confidently.

"Yoo-hoo!" came Mira's voice.

"Oh no," groaned Teggs. "I didn't mean *him*!"

"Hello?" The liopleurodon was getting closer. "Where are you?"

The two astrosaurs ducked down behind some clumps of seaweed.

"The ghosts have gone!" he shouted. "You can come back now!" Then his mouth opened in a big smile. "Oh, I see! It's a game! Hide and seek! Can't we play hunt the spaceship instead? I know it's round here somewhere . . ."

Mira swam closer, his massive head searching this way and that. Soon he would find them.

"Run for it!" hissed Teggs.

Together, the two astrosaurs sprinted through the murky water. They slipped on slimy seaweed. Coral scraped their legs. Their sides ached with effort.

"Found you!" cried Mira, behind them. "You can't hide from me!"

"We have to keep going," gasped Teggs.

There was a big patch of slimy seaweed ahead. They slipped and skidded over it. Then, with a shout, Teggs fell *through* the seaweed!

Gipsy grabbed hold of his vanishing tail. She tried to pull him back up, but he was too heavy.

With a cry, Gipsy was dragged down through the slimy seaweed after him, into the blackness beyond.

The fall lasted only a few seconds. Teggs went tumbling through the water until he landed on his bottom with a bump. Gipsy landed beside him a second later. They were in a wide tunnel. Although the walls were thick with limpets and seaweed, something shiny was glinting through underneath.

Teggs took a closer look. "This isn't rock. It's metal!" he cried.

"A metal tunnel under the seabed?" Gipsy frowned. "What could it be?"

"Let's find out," he said. The astrosaurs walked cautiously along the tunnel, straining to see through the murky water. Then they came to a doorway. A sign glowed eerily above them:

CONTROL ROOM.

Teggs nodded gravely. "I think we're inside a spaceship!"

"*Mira's* spaceship!" gasped Gipsy. "The one he's trying to find! But what's it doing here?"

"He didn't *park* it under the water," Teggs realized. "He must have *crashed* it into the ocean and right through the sea bed! I think we fell in through a big hole in the roof, hidden by the seaweed."

"But how do we get back out?" wondered Gipsy. "There's no way we can climb out of that hole again! And a search party would never think of looking for us down here. They don't even know this place exists!"

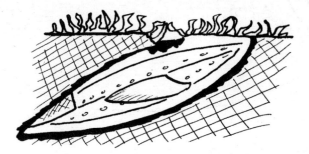

"And on top of all that, our air is running out fast," said Teggs. "Come on, Gipsy. Let's try to find another way back to the sea bed. . ."

Cautiously, they crept on into the gloomy spaceship's control room.

Chapter Seven

A TOOTHY RIDDLE

The sunken spaceship's control room was large and wide with a low ceiling. It was clearly designed for giant sea creatures. The controls were built into the floor, so the crew could work them with their tails and flippers.

Gipsy looked at a plastic newspaper floating in the water "*The Liopleurodon Times*. It's six years old!" she said. "This ship has been down here for six whole years at the very least!"

"So the ship crashed here a year before the cryptoclidus first arrived," Teggs realized. "And the trouble only started when they started building factories around this area."

"Maybe they disturbed something," said Gipsy. "Something dangerous!" Teggs nodded. Then he noticed a metal box on the floor with an aerial on top, half covered by the water. "Hey, Gipsy! This looks familiar . . ."

"It's for sending distress calls!" cried Gipsy. "We've got something like it on the *Sauropod*." She looked closely at the box. "It's broken. But maybe I can fix it!"

"Try!" Teggs urged her. "If we could only send an SOS to Sea Station One . . ."

He waited anxiously while Gipsy went to work with her delicate claws. Finally she gave a small hoot of success. "I think I've got it working," she said. "But there's not much power. The signal is very weak."

"Someone will hear it," said Teggs quietly. "They *must*."

With nothing to do but wait, the astrosaurs moved on into the cold shadows of the creepy ship.

Meanwhile, back on Sea Station One, Iggy and Arx were hard at work down in the storeroom. The two of them had been waiting ages for news of Teggs and Gipsy. They were worried sick.

Arx was still checking over the chewed-up wreckage. He was patiently comparing sections of sub, fragments of floating factory and bits of the diving bell.

Iggy had talked some cryptoclidus sailors into helping him fix one of the broken subs. They were busy in the room next door, hammering out dents in the sub's metal body and fixing all the instruments. Iggy himself had taken tiny pieces from all the subs and was using them to build a brand new engine. Now it was ready for testing, so he switched it on.

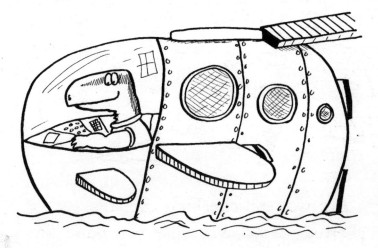

With a gentle hum, the engine started up first time.

"I've done it!" cried Iggy. "This new engine is ten times better and fifty times quieter than the old ones!"

Then the door to the storeroom flew open as Cripes splashed inside.

Arx and Iggy spoke together. "Well?"

"The search party can't find a thing down there," said Cripes. "But every radio in the place is picking up some kind of weird SOS call! It seems to be coming from somewhere *beneath* the sea bed!"

"It *might* be Teggs and Gipsy," cried Arx.

"If they are down there, I'll find them!" vowed Iggy. "My new super-sub is almost ready to go. And it's fitted with all kinds of extra gadgets!"

"But we know that the liopleurodon has a taste for subs," Cripes reminded him. "It chomped all the old ones to pieces!"

Arx cleared his throat. "Actually, that's not true."

Cripes and Iggy stared at him.

"It was not a liopleurodon who chomped up the subs," he went on. "And it was not a liopleurodon who wrecked those floating factories."

"Come on!" Cripes scoffed. "You'll be telling us next that a liopleurodon didn't chew up that diving bell."

"Oh, no," said Arx. "A liopleurodon *definitely* did that." He nodded. "That's how I know it didn't do anything else!"

"How?" asked Cripes.

"Tooth marks!" cried Arx. "Look at that diving bell. It was ripped apart by long, sharp teeth. You can see the marks from here."

"So?" said Iggy.

"So, I haven't found tooth marks like that anywhere else," Arx said.

"Not on *any* of this wreckage."

"What *did* you find?" asked Cripes.

"*Tiny* marks," Arx told him. "Hundreds of thousands of tiny little marks – made by tiny little teeth!"

"But that's impossible," protested Iggy. "You and Captain Teggs both saw a huge shadow in the sea. That has to be the liopleurodon, right?"

"Maybe not," said Arx. "Maybe the liopleurodon is working with something else. Something just as big . . . or maybe even bigger!"

Cripes took off his hat and scratched his head with a flipper. "Strange for something so big to have such teeny-weeny teeth."

"Never mind all that," said Iggy. "Let's get going!" He patted his shiny new engine. "We'll find Captain Teggs and Gipsy. And we'll find whatever else is hiding down there in the deeps, too – whatever it takes!"

Chapter Eight

THE FISH FACTOR

Back beneath the sea bed, Teggs and Gipsy were still exploring the liopleurodon ship. It was cold, dark and scary. And both of them knew that their precious air supply was running out with every breath they took. As they walked along one dark corridor, the dirty water grew chillier. Slowly it was becoming a thick, icy slush.

"Shall we turn back?" asked Gipsy nervously. "We don't want to wind up as dinosaur ice-pops!"

"Just a little further," said Teggs.

The chilly passage ended in what seemed to be a giant freezer. Lying in the middle of the room were four big caskets made of solid ice. Teggs could see the huge dark shape of a liopleurodon lying inside three of them. But the fourth was damaged. Part of the ceiling had collapsed on top of it, and the casket had cracked right open.

"This must be Mira's crew," Gipsy gasped. "Are they dead?"

"Just sleeping, I think," breathed Teggs. "A deep, frozen sleep to keep them fresh while they wait to be rescued. But Mira's woken up ahead of time!"

Gipsy pointed to some blue scraps in the water beside the broken casket. "What are they?"

"Bits of Mira's uniform I think. There's writing on them." Teggs took a closer look. "A and D on this bit. An L on the other. What does that mean?"

"Admiral!" cried Gipsy.

Teggs frowned. "I'm only a captain at the moment!"

"No, I'm talking about Mira!" Gipsy's crest flushed red with excitement, and made her helmet steam up. "He thought his name was Mira because it's written on that scrap of uniform he wears. But that's only *part* of the word. Really it spells AD—MIRA—L!"

"Of course!" breathed Teggs. "Then this really *is* his ship. But the ceiling fell in on his head before he could get into the deep freeze. That must be how he lost his memory!"

"Poor Mira," sighed Gipsy. "He must've slipped out into the sea in a daze, and forgotten how to get back!"

"Yes — and something else may have slipped out with him," said Teggs quietly. "Let's keep looking."

"I wonder how much longer our air will last," said Gipsy quietly. "We can't have much left by now."

"I know," said Teggs. "But we mustn't give up. An astrosaur fights on to the last breath!" He paused. "Sorry, that wasn't a very clever thing to say, was it?"

They left the chilly chamber and took a side-tunnel. Soon they

came to another room. It was marked
LARDER – DO NOT DISTURB. A
huge aquarium stretched along one wall
for hundreds of metres. Nothing moved
in the eerie, dark water.

"This must be where their food lived,"
said Gipsy.

Teggs was puzzled. "Strange to have
an aquarium in a ship that's already full
of water."

"I suppose the fish would swim all
over the ship otherwise, trying to escape
being eaten," Gipsy guessed. Then she
noticed a big hole in the back of the
tank. "Captain! The fish *did* escape!
Look, they must have swum away into
the sea!"

"Good for them," smiled Teggs. "I'm
glad they got out." A thought struck
him. "And if they did, maybe so can
we! If we could find our way back out
to the sea bed, a search party might
spot us!"

"Brilliant!" cried Gipsy.

"All we have to do is break the glass . . ."
He struck the side of the tank with his
tail. The glass glowed a brilliant blue and
a crack appeared in its centre.

But suddenly an alarm went off at ear-
splitting volume. Steel bars slammed
down to block the doorway. They were
trapped inside the larder.

"What did I do?" cried Teggs.

The siren stopped as a helpful computer voice chimed in from a speaker in the ceiling: "You tried to open the fish tank without a password. You are an intruder and a fish-pincher."

Teggs stared up at the speaker. "What would I do with a fish? I'm a vegetarian!"

"A likely story!" snarled the computer. The siren switched on again, only this time it was even louder.

"But there aren't even any fish in the tank!" yelled Teggs.

"Oh yes, there are," said Gipsy. A few deep blue fish had swum inside through the big hole. They came up to the front of the tank, as if to see what was happening. A few others came to join them. Then more. And more. Soon there

were hundreds of fish staring at Gipsy
through the glass.

They didn't seem very happy.

"Turn that siren off!" yelled Teggs. He
tried to bang his tail against the speaker
– but it was just out of reach.

"No way!" snapped the computer.
"I'm going to turn it *up*!" Sure enough,
the siren grew louder still.

"My ears are going to burst!" groaned Teggs. He bashed the steel bars with his tail. They sparked, but held firm. "We can't get out!"

"Never mind *us* getting *out*," said Gipsy fearfully. "Let's just hope those fish can't get *in*!"

"Fish? Why are you bothered about a few fish . . .?"

But Teggs trailed off when he looked at the aquarium.

There were thousands of the tiny creatures now. They had banded together into one enormous group – a huge huddle of angry blue fish, moving and acting as one.

Floating all together, they made Mira seem like a minnow.

"That's the same shape I saw back at the floating factory," Teggs cried over the ear-splitting noise. "It wasn't a giant monster who sank the subs and chewed up the factories after all. It was these

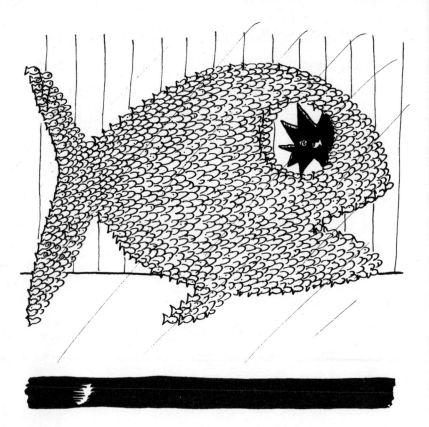

little fish – working together to *act* like
a giant monster!"

Suddenly the dark, seething shape
swept forwards and smashed into the
glass like a living battering ram.

"And now they want to get in here!"
cried Gipsy.

"But why?" wondered Teggs. "What have we done?"

The thousands of fish opened their little mouths and gnashed at the glass. The crack in the side of the tank grew wider.

"Their teeth are as sharp as sharks'!" gasped Gipsy. "I think they're going to eat *us*!"

Chapter Nine

FIN-ISHED?

The great mass of the little blue fish attacked the side of the tank again. The crack spread into a pattern of crazy zigzags, stretching from floor to ceiling.

"Look out, Gipsy!" shouted Teggs. "They're coming through!"

The fish hurled themselves at the glass, and the tank burst open. Teggs and Gipsy watched helplessly as the tiny creatures swarmed inside the larder . . .

. . . and ignored them completely.

Instead, the fish headed for the speaker in the ceiling, attacking it and tearing it open with their vicious teeth.

The sound of the siren faded.

"Under attack!" gasped the computer voice. "The whisperfish have escaped the larder! Assistance needed—"

Then with a flash of sparks and an electronic cough, the voice and the siren shut off all together.

Teggs' and Gipsy's ears rang in the sudden silence.

And, the next second, the "monster" vanished as all the fish swam swiftly away in different directions. A few of them hung about in the larder, their little mouths opening and closing. But the rest were already swimming back out to sea as if nothing had ever happened.

"Of course!" yelled Teggs at the top of his voice. But some of the fish gave him a nasty look, so he quickly shut up. "They weren't after us. They were after whatever was making the noise!"

"I don't get it," frowned Gipsy.

"You were right," he went on. "The cryptoclidus did disturb something when they built their factories here in the south – those whisperfish! Whisperfish must *hate* noise!"

Gipsy nodded slowly. "Well, the glass in that tank was very thick," she said. "I'll bet it made things ever so quiet in there."

"And once the ship crashed and they escaped, the ocean must have been quiet too," Teggs went on. "Until the cryptoclidus started building in whisperfish waters!"

"Of course!"
cried Gipsy.
"Ever since
then, these
whisperfish
have been
joining together
to chew up
anything that
makes a loud noise
– floating factories . . .
submarines . . . that silly siren . . . And
once they've stopped the racket, they
split up again."

"And so the 'monster'
seems to vanish!"
Teggs nodded.
"That's why the
whisperfish left us
alone in our nice
quiet shuttle and the
silent diving bell. We
weren't disturbing them!"

214

"Well, now we know what's been going on," said Gipsy. "But what good does it do us? We're almost out of air."

Teggs nodded. He felt a bit dizzy. "If we're not rescued soon . . ."

As he spoke, a massive, dark shape swam up to them through the shattered tank.

"Oh no," groaned Teggs.

It was Mira!

"Coo-eee!" he said, waving a flipper. "I've been looking everywhere for you two! Now, it's my turn to hide . . ." he tailed off. "Wait a moment. This is my spaceship! What are you doing inside my spaceship?"

"Trying to get out!" cried Gipsy.

But then a bright yellow light shone in at them through the glass.

"Don't tell me it's *another* monster!" Teggs groaned.

"It's . . . it's some kind of super submarine!" gasped Gipsy in surprise.

A gleaming sub was gliding through the water towards them.

Mira spun round to see. Then he scowled. "It's those flipper-flappers!" he shouted. "They want to catch us! Well, I'll show them a thing or two!"

With that, he streaked out of the tank and over to the sub. His jaws were open wide.

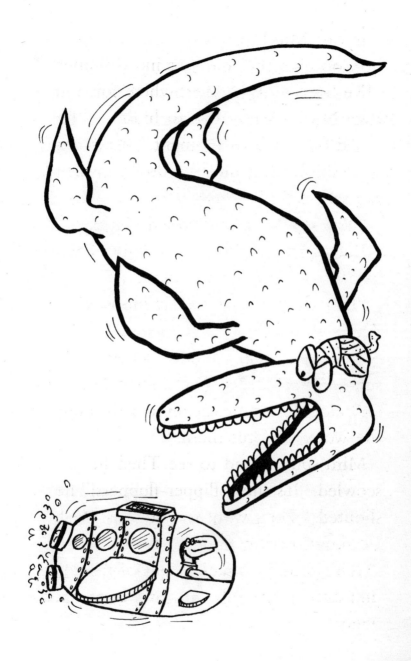

Teggs stared in horror. "No, Mira, don't!"

But as Mira bit down on the nose of the sub – *Zzzzap!*

His eyes bulged. Then he stuck out his tongue, closed his eyes and fell quietly to the sea bed.

A hatch opened on top of the sub and Cripes swam out!

Gipsy hugged Teggs with relief.

"So you *did* hear our SOS signal," smiled Teggs weakly.

Cripes nodded. "Arx worked out the best way to reach you, and Iggy drove us here in record time!" He frowned. "Uh, you're looking kind of . . . blue!"

"We're nearly out of air," gasped Teggs.

"I think I'm going to faint," croaked
Gipsy.

"Quick!" cried Cripes. "Into the sub!"

With the last of their strength, Teggs
and Gipsy made it aboard. Cripes shut
the doors and led them out of the
water. Gipsy wriggled out of her helmet
and gulped down air. Teggs just swung
his head into the wall and broke the
glass helmet like an oversized egg.

"That's better!" he whooped. "And
have *we* got a story to tell you!"

"Tell me about it when you have had
a rest," said Cripes gently. "You two
have been through a lot!"

"What happened to Mira?" asked
Gipsy.

"He'll be all right," said Cripes. "He's just sleeping. When Iggy fixed up the sub, he also gave it a special force field!"

"Of course," beamed Teggs. "A force field's like a wall of solid energy. When Mira tried to bite it, he got a big shock!"

"Poor Mira," sighed Gipsy. "He's not really bad."

"We'll tow him back to Sea Station One," Teggs declared. "Then we can work out how to get him back home."

The sub's inner door opened and Iggy peered in. "Captain! Gipsy!" he beamed with delight. "You're all right!"

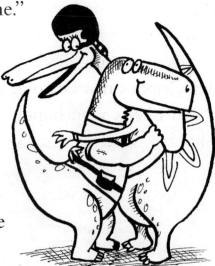

220

"Just about," sighed Gipsy. She gave Iggy a hug. "Though it's going to take *weeks* to get all the wrinkles out of my skin!"

A few hours later, the astrosaurs were safely back aboard Sea Station One. Teggs and Gipsy were both chilled through from spending so long in the freezing sea. But after a lovely hot bath and a bucket of warm sea-grass, they started to feel a bit better.

The sleeping Mira had been towed to a special undersea pen. The pen was locked, and Cripes had placed guards there. A few hours later, the astrosaurs met Cripes on a balcony above the pen.

"No one is very happy about having a liopleurodon here at Sea Station One," grumbled Cripes.

"If he meant you any harm, don't you think he'd have attacked you already?" said Gipsy.

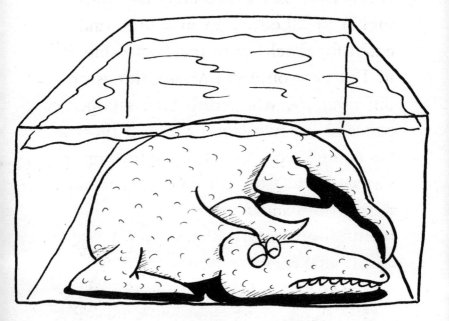

"I guess so," said Cripes. "Speaking of attacks, thanks for finding the truth behind our mysterious monster! Now all we have to do is catch all the whisperfish and they'll never bother us again!"

Teggs gave Cripes a hard stare. "That doesn't seem fair."

"What do you mean?" asked Cripes.

"It can't be much fun being a

whisperfish on the liopleurodon world," said Teggs. "Locked up in a tank and eaten for lunch – not much of a life, is it? But here on Aqua Minor, things are different. The whisperfish have enjoyed a peaceful life swimming freely in the sea for years." Teggs marched angrily up to Cripes. "And what do you want to do now? You want to catch them all and send them back home for supper!"

"But they're dangerous!" Cripes complained.

"All they want is some peace and quiet," said Arx. "They've never bothered you in the north. They

probably won't bother you in the east and the west, either."

"Share the planet with them, Cripes," Teggs urged him. "Let them live here in peace."

Cripes nodded, a little shamefaced. "You're right. I'm sorry. Of course we'll let them stay!"

"HEY!" came a booming voice from the undersea pen. "What's going on here?"

"It's Mira!" said Teggs. "He's woken up!"

"But he sounds different," said Gipsy. "He sounds really scary!"

Suddenly Mira crashed through the surface of the water and glared up at them. "Who are you?" he bawled. "Who dares to lock *me* up?"

"Don't you recognize us?" said Gipsy.

"Never seen you before!" he shouted. "I'm hungry! What have you done with my whisperfish?"

"They're off the menu," Teggs told him. "Sorry!"

"Sorry? You will be!" snarled the liopleurodon. "I'm Admiral Don Leo of the Liopleurodon Space Fleet! The last thing I remember was crash-landing on this crummy planet during a test flight." His eyes narrowed. "But now I've woken up. And I'm hungry. And I'm very, *very* ANGRY!"

Chapter Ten

ALL WRAPPED UP!

Arx cleared his throat. "It would seem that the liopleurodon's memory has come back," he said. "It must be the shock he got from biting the force field!"

"No one keeps me locked up!" roared Don Leo. "Forget the whisperfish – I'll eat every one of *you* when I get out of here!"

"Oh, dear," sighed Teggs. "We've dealt with one monster. Now here's another one to take its place!"

"There's not a prison built that can hold me!" growled Don Leo. "And I'll prove it!" He swam at top speed towards the side of the pen and bashed it over and over. The wall was thick, but soon cracks were starting to show.

Cripes was trembling. "He's going to get out into the open sea! Think of the damage he could cause!"

"We'll just have to stop him," said Teggs simply. "Cripes, Iggy, let's head for the super-sub – fast!"

With a final roar of rage, Don Leo smashed a huge hole in the side of the pen.

"Now I'm going to eat everyone on this planet!" he yelled.

"Not so fast!" shouted Teggs from the super-sub. "First you'll have to deal with a couple of astrosaurs!"

With that, Iggy turned the super-sub round and revved the dung-powered engines right in Don Leo's furious face.

"That tastes revolting!" Don Leo spluttered. "I'll get you for that!"

The super-sub sped away, the liopleurodon close behind it.

"All right, Cripes," said Teggs. "Where's the nearest floating factory?"

"About three miles north," said Cripes. "But it's a brand new building. We've only just put all the machines in."

"Perfect!" cried Teggs. "Well away from the whisperfish. Iggy, get us there at top speed!"

"Aye-aye, Captain," grinned Iggy. But though the super-sub soared through the saltwater at an incredible speed, Don Leo was catching up!

"We *must* keep ahead of him, Iggy!" urged Teggs.

Cripes pointed to a big block of metal ahead of them. "There's the floating factory!"

"Does it have a packing room?" asked Teggs. "You know, like the one I got trapped in on the wreck?"

"Sure it does," said Cripes. "Iggy, head for the intake pipe round the side. It'll take you straight there. But I still don't see—"

"No time for explanations now," said Teggs, as they shot through the pipe and into the loading area. "I'm getting off! Park the sub and wait for me."

"But Don Leo's right behind us!" protested Iggy. "If he sees you, he'll eat you!"

"I hope he *tries*," smiled Teggs. "My plan depends on it!"

Iggy parked the super-sub just outside the packing room. As it bobbed about on the surface of the water, Teggs jumped out and quickly waded over to another large pipe, half-filled with water. Designed to let through tons of shelled ammonites for packing, it was easily big enough to fit a stegosaurus.

And, with a bit of a squeeze, a livid liopleurodon.

Don Leo suddenly burst out of the water beside Teggs, ready to bite. His terrifying teeth missed Teggs's neck by millimetres.

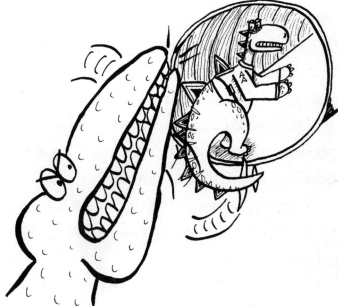

"Phew!" whistled Teggs. "You know, I think I liked Mira a whole lot better than Don Leo!"

"I'll like you a whole lot better when you're lining my stomach!" growled Don Leo.

"Don't hold your breath," said Teggs. He bashed Don Leo on the nose with his tail.

"Come here!" Don Leo roared in anger.

Teggs waded off down the pipe, with the liopleurodon slithering along right behind him, trying to squeeze through.

A few seconds later, Teggs splashed out into the packing room. Panting for breath, he turned on the machines. The conveyor belt jerked forwards. Metal scoops swung down from the ceiling.

Don Leo wriggled along through the shallow water after Teggs. He looked *furious*.

"Catch me if you can!" cried Teggs.

He climbed up onto the clanking
conveyor belt.

"I'll chase you onto dry land if I have
to!" snarled Don Leo. Somehow he
managed to flip himself out of the
water and onto the conveyor belt
behind Teggs.

Now they were both heading straight
for the wrapping machine.

Don Leo laughed nastily. "I've got
you now, you stupid stegosaur!"

Teggs just smiled. "Actually, I think you'll find that . . . *I've got you!*"

Just before he could fall into the wrapping machine, Teggs jumped off the conveyor belt. He hit the water with an enormous splash. But it was too late for Don Leo. He couldn't flip himself out of the way in time.

"No!" yelled the liopleurodon as he tumbled into the wrapping machine.

Teggs held his breath as the machine rattled and shook. Then it bulged like a balloon. Steam started to spurt from its insides.

Finally, out popped Don Leo, all wrapped up on a long plastic tray. Only his head, tail and flippers were left sticking out.

"Get me out of here!" yelled the liopleurodon, struggling furiously.

But the conveyor belt moved him quickly on. He was tipped into a large wooden crate. Robot arms placed the lid on top and nailed it in place. Finally the crate was shoved off into the water with a big splash.

"There," said Teggs. "That should hold you till you've calmed down a bit!"

"What about my ship?" came Don Leo's muffled voice.

"I think your test flight is over," said Teggs. "That ship will never fly again. But your crew are still safely sleeping. If you promise to be good, I'm sure the cryptoclidus will help you all get back home to your own planet."

"And what if we're *not* good?" said Don Leo.

"I was sent here by the Dinosaur Space Service. They'll be watching you very closely," Teggs said sternly. "If you know what's good for you . . . behave!"

Just then, Iggy and Cripes splashed into the packing room.

"You did it!" beamed Iggy.

"At last, we can get on with our fishing in peace," said Cripes.

"As soon as you've helped Don Leo and his friends get back home," said Teggs. "But don't worry. I think he'll be better behaved from now on!"

"Suppose so," grumbled Don Leo from his crate.

"Well, I think that about *wraps things up* here," chuckled Teggs. He spoke into his communicator. "Arx? Gipsy? It's Teggs. Mission accomplished!"

Gipsy's voice crackled out: "Well done, Captain!"

"Admiral Rosso will be delighted!" added Arx.

"Get the shuttle ready," Teggs ordered. "Then let's all grab dinner somewhere *dry*." He grinned at Iggy. "I'm ready for a ten course banquet – with a big, new adventure for dessert!"

THE END

TALKING DINOSAUR!

TRICERATOPS –
try-SERRA-tops

STEGOSAURUS –
STEG-oh-SORE-us

BAROSAURUS –
bar-oh-SORE-us

IGUANODON –
ig-WA-noh-don

HADROSAUR –
HAD-roh-sore

DIMORPHODON –
die-MORF-oh-don

CRYPTOCLIDUS –
cript-oh-CLIE-dus

LIOPLEURODON –
LIE-oh-PLUR-oh-don

THE
SKIES
OF
FEAR

By Steve Cole

Illustrated by
Woody Fox

For Matthew and Andrew

Chapter One

THE LONG SQUAWK

It was midnight on board
the DSS *Sauropod*.
All was quiet as the
ship soared through
space.

A few astrosaurs
were working late.
Ankylosaurs tinkered
with the ship's mighty
engines. Stygimolochs mopped and
cleaned the corridors. The alarm
pterosaur made a cup of swamp tea to
help her stay awake.

And then a strange sound started up.
It was a weird, straining *ROAR* of a

sound. Like a T. rex trying to lay a two-ton egg. Like a thousand chickens singing from the bottom of a well. Like a billion beaks bashing at a battleship.

The sound blared from the *Sauropod's* speakers all round the ship. The ankylosaurs dropped their tools in surprise. The shocked  stygimolochs threw their mops and buckets in the air. The alarm pterosaur screeched but no one could hear her over the dreadful din.

Captain Teggs Stegosaur jumped out of bed and galloped to the nearest lift, still in his pyjamas. He was a dashing, orange-brown stegosaurus who feared nothing – except perhaps an empty larder. For Teggs, the best things in life were eating and having adventures, ideally at the same time. But being woken at midnight by a sinister sound was enough to make even *him* lose his appetite.

As he reached the lift he saw that Gipsy Saurine had got there ahead of him. This bright stripy hadrosaur was in charge of the *Sauropod*'s communications. She took her hooves from her ears to salute him.

"Never mind that," Teggs told her. "If my hands could *reach* my ears, I'd cover them too! We've got to stop that terrible noise!"

"I'm sure the dimorphodon are working out what's going on right now," said Gipsy.

The dimorphodon, a type of pterosaur, were the *Sauropod*'s flight crew. There were fifty of the little flying reptiles on duty right now. With their nimble claws and delicate beaks they worked the ship's controls swiftly and surely.

Or rather, they *usually* did.

As Teggs and Gipsy burst out of the lift and onto the flight deck, they found the dimorphodon were standing as still as statues.

"What can have happened to them?" cried Gipsy.

"Quick, shut off the speakers," Teggs told her. "I think my ears are about to explode!"

Gipsy rushed to her post and pressed a button. A sudden silence fell over the flight deck. Then the lift doors swished open and a green triceratops burst in. It was Arx Orano, Teggs's first officer. He had dressed so quickly, he'd forgotten to take off his nightcap.

"Are we under attack?" he gasped.

"I don't know!" Teggs turned to Gipsy. "Any sign of enemy ships?"

"None, sir." She peered closely at her instruments. "The signal is coming from a long way away . . ."

"See if you can pinpoint the source of it," Teggs ordered. He was inspecting the dimorphodon. Their little eyes were goggly and glazed, and their beaks hung open.

"They're in some kind of trance," said Arx, sad to see his flapping friends in such a state. "That sound – perhaps it's some kind of weapon!"

"But *we* haven't been affected." Teggs frowned. "Have we?"

Just then, Iggy Tooth stomped out of the lift. Iggy was a stocky iguanodon, the *Sauropod*'s chief engineer. He was also very good in a fight – and it looked like he was ready for one now!

"I was having a brilliant dream about beating the raptors in a space-car race," he grumbled. "Then that nasty noise made me fall out of bed! What *was* it?"

"We're trying to find out," said Teggs, crossing to Gipsy's side. "But first I'd better talk to the crew!"

"Good idea," Iggy agreed. "After a scare like that, we'll have enough extra dung on board to power the ship for a whole month!"

Gipsy flicked a switch and Teggs's voice boomed over the rattling speakers. "This is your captain! Don't panic. Everything is under control."

But suddenly the flight crew snapped back into life. They squealed and squawked and flapped all around, working the controls at top speed.

"What's got into them?" gasped Gipsy.

The floor lurched beneath their feet. "We're changing course!" said Arx.

"Stop it!" shouted Teggs. "We're on our way to meet Admiral Rosso at DSS Headquarters! You can't just steer us somewhere else!"

But the dimorphodon wouldn't listen.

Gipsy was astounded. "They've never disobeyed an order before!"

"*I'll* sort them out," said Iggy. He jumped up and grabbed the dimorphodon team leader – a plucky little reptile they nicknamed Sprite. "Stop that flapping and explain yourself!"

Sprite wriggled in Iggy's hands. He chittered and squeaked.

Gipsy spoke fluent pterosaur, and so she quickly translated. "He says that the sound we all heard was the Long Squawk."

"The *what*?" asked Teggs.

Again, Sprite clucked and squealed. The rest of the dimorphodon waited in mid-air, but Teggs could see they were dying to get on.

"The Long Squawk is a special signal, only sent in an extreme emergency," Gipsy explained. "It's an urgent summons from the High Flapper!"

"The *who*?" asked Teggs.

"The ruler of Squawk Major, the pterosaurs' home planet," said Arx. "Whatever's happening, Captain, it must be pretty serious. The Long Squawk hasn't been heard for two hundred years. When they hear the signal, all pterosaurs – whatever their breed, wherever they are – must return home at once."

"Return home at once!" cried the

alarm pterosaur over the speakers. "Full speed ahead! Return home at once!"

"I see what you mean!" said Teggs.

"I've traced the source of the sound, Captain," Gipsy reported. "It *is* coming from Squawk Major."

"The High Flapper must need help very badly," said Arx.

Sprite gave a sad little cheep.

Teggs nodded. "All right, Iggy, let Sprite go."

Sprite fluttered free with a grateful smile.

"And get your team to shovel all that fresh dung straight into the engines," Teggs continued. "We'll need it if we're going to stay at top speed all the way to Squawk Major."

Iggy saluted. "Right away, Captain!"

At once, the dimorphodon flapped back into action, working the *Sauropod*'s controls while Arx supervised.

"Won't Admiral Rosso be cross with

us?" wondered Gipsy.

"I'm sure he'll understand," said Teggs. "It sounds like this is a real emergency." He chomped on a beakful of ferns and smiled at the thought of a new adventure. "There's no time to lose!"

Chapter Two

IN A FLAP

As it turned out, Admiral Rosso was glad the *Sauropod* was already speeding to Squawk Major.

"You're captain of our fastest ship, Teggs," the old barosaurus remarked. "As soon as I heard the Long Squawk, I planned to send you there. You must help Lady Shazz, the High Flapper, in any way you can!"

Iggy was pleased too, once he'd had a nap. "Squawk Major is the planet next door to Morass Minor," he said. "They hold the Mammoth Space-Car Rally there every month."

Arx didn't know much about sport. "Do you mean 'mammoth' as in really big, or 'mammoth' as in large, woolly elephant-thing with tusks?"

"Both!" grinned Iggy. "Once we've sorted out this flap with the pterosaurs, maybe we could pop across and watch the races!"

"Maybe," said Teggs. He was worried. Lady Shazz had refused to say what was wrong until they could talk face to face.

"Approaching Squawk Major now, Captain," said Arx.

"A ptero-taxi just called," Gipsy added. "They're ready to pick us up,"

Teggs clambered out of his control pit. "Time to go,' he said. "But first, Gipsy, put a call through to Alass."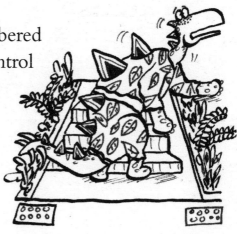

"Connecting you now, sir," she told him.

"Yes, Captain?" asked Alass, as her face appeared on the main screen. She was the ankylosaurus in charge of security.

Teggs smiled. "Since the dimorphodon are coming to Squawk Major with Gipsy, Arx, Iggy and me, I'm leaving you in charge until we get back."

Alass gave him her
smartest salute.
"Understood, sir!"
"Right, then," Teggs
told the rest of his crew.
"Let's take that taxi!"

Spaceships were banned from the
skies of Squawk Major. The planet's air
was pure and fresh, and smelly engines
would spoil it for the millions of
pterosaurs flying happily through the
sweet-smelling skies. So any visitors

wanting to land on the planet had to leave their spaceship in orbit and take a ptero-taxi – a special space-carriage pulled by a team of pterosaurs.

Teggs, Arx, Gipsy and Iggy all squeezed on board. The dimorphodon and the alarm pterosaur flapped in after them. Then the shuttle bay doors swung open, and the two drivers – a pair of rugged nyctosaurus in spacesuits – flapped off into space, towing the taxi behind them.

Squawk Major
lay below them
like a giant
orange
pudding,
streaked
with wisps
of creamy
white cloud.
A little tear of
joy trickled
down the alarm
pterosaur's beak at the sight of her
home.

Soon they were soaring through the
rosy skies.

"Where is everybody?" Teggs
wondered. "This is a planet of flying
reptiles. But I don't see anyone flying!"

"Maybe we're too high up," Gipsy
suggested.

But as the minutes passed, the skies
stayed empty. Sprite chirped worriedly.

262

The alarm pterosaur patted him on the head with her wing.

"We're only three miles above the ground," Arx reported. "It should be quite busy round here by now."

"Look on the bright side," said Iggy. "At least with an empty sky we can't possibly crash into anything!"

But suddenly, there were two noisy squawks from outside.

"What's happening?" cried Gipsy.

"The pilots!" Teggs pointed to the nyctosaurus through the window. "They've stopped flapping!"

At once, the ptero-taxi dropped like a stone.

"They'd better *start* flapping, and fast!" said Iggy.

The nyctosaurus screeched loudly.

"They can't!" cried Gipsy. "They – they say they've *forgotten* how to fly!"

"Forgotten?" Arx gulped. "How can that be? They were fine a minute ago!"

The carriage was falling faster and faster.

"If they don't remember soon, we'll all be squashed flat!" cried Iggy. "And so will anyone beneath us!"

"We've got one chance," said Teggs. He whacked his spiny tail against the window and smashed out the glass. "Dimorphodon – take over!"

At once, Sprite led the valiant flight crew outside. Flying against the wind, they managed to take control of the

taxi from the
helpless
nyctosaurus. The
dimorphodon
were far smaller,
of course, but
there were fifty of
them. They started
flapping for their lives
– and the lives of their captain
and crew!

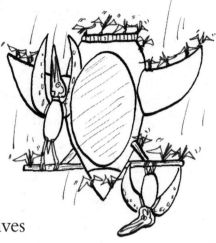

"We're slowing down!" gasped Arx.
"But not fast enough!"

Gipsy shut her eyes as the ground
came rushing up to meet them.

Then the alarm pterosaur, who was
not the bravest of flying reptiles,
hopped out through the window.
Flapping furiously, she lent her wings
to the struggle.

With a rush of relief, Teggs felt the
carriage coming back under control.
"They're doing it!"

"Thank goodness," beamed Gipsy, as the flock of pterosaurs towed them onwards. "We're going to be all right!"

Iggy wiped his brow. "And I'm going to keep my mouth shut for the rest of the trip!"

But Arx was still lost in thought. "How can a pterosaur forget how to fly? That's like Captain Teggs forgetting how to eat!"

"Pardon?" said Teggs through a mouthful of ferns.

The nyctosaurus could no longer fly, but at least they could give directions. Puffing and panting, the dimorphodon and the alarm pterosaur steered the carriage to the majestic home of the High Flapper – the Palace of Perches.

It towered over the castles and courtyards of the pterosaur city. It was beautifully built from bright blue rock, and was as big as a cathedral. Hundreds of stone flagpoles jutted from the walls, which were covered in carvings of beasts and birds.

"There's no door," said Teggs. "How do we get in?"

"Through the roof!" said Arx.

They circled overhead and swooped down through a large hole in the great glass ceiling. Inside, was a single, enormous room, filled with fruit trees and flowers. And there, right in the middle, sat the enormous Lady Shazz, the High Flapper.

Perched on a giant purple cushion, she was a regal sight: a crown upon her head, her long beak raised skyward, her leathery wings stretched out wider than a jet plane.

The ptero-taxi touched down beside

her. At once, servants flapped over with cool drinks and insects for the exhausted pilots.

Teggs led the others from the carriage, and bowed. "Greetings, your Highness."

"Greetings, astrosaurs," trilled Shazz. (Being the High Flapper, she spoke fluent dinosaur.) "Thank you for coming all this way."

"We would have got here sooner,"
said Teggs. "But halfway here, your
pilots forgot how to fly!"

"Oh no!" Shazz slumped back onto
her cushion. "Not them too! My last
pair of plucky pilots!"

Arx frowned.
"You mean this
has happened
before?"

"It's been happening
for weeks!" she sighed. "Every day,
millions more of us forget how to fly!"

She gave a miserable squawk and
buried her beak in her
massive wings.

"However hard
they try, they
simply can't
remember how
to do it!"

Chapter Three

THE COMING OF GRANDUM

"So that's why the skies are empty," Iggy realized.

Gipsy couldn't believe it. "But they're pterosaurs! Surely they can learn how to fly again?"

"They've tried and tried but they just can't get the hang of it." Shazz shed a silvery tear. "This morning, I thought I would fly over and teach some of them myself. But I fell flat on my face! Even *I* have forgotten how to fly! A High Flapper without her flap!" She wiped her long beak on an even longer wing. "And as if all this wasn't bad enough, the Trials are almost due to start!"

271

"Trials?" asked Teggs.

"The High Flapper Trials!" Shazz wailed. "I have ruled Squawk Major for almost ten years. According to pterosaur law, it is time for a new High Flapper to be chosen. A special contest will be held on Beak Mountain in one week's time. It is open to all flying reptiles. They will compete for the crown in trials of skill, strength and speed . . . But so far, not one person has entered!"

Arx nodded. "Because none of them can fly!"

"That is why I sent the Long Squawk alarm call into space," Shazz explained. "I have called back pterosaurs from all over the Jurassic Quadrant to take part!"

The dimorphodon and the alarm pterosaur squawked in surprise.

"And here comes one now!" cried Gipsy. "Look! Up there!"

A dark cloud had gathered over the palace, and an even darker shape was swooping out of it. It was an enormous flying reptile, the size of an elephant. Its wings were like huge hairy sheets, and bigger than a jumbo jet's. Its body was broad and fat. Its head was long and leathery with a big, bent beak.

Whoosh! It dropped right in through the skylight!

"What a cheek!" gasped Shazz.

"What a *pong!*" Teggs complained. The

273

new arrival stank of dung and grease and engine oil. "I could smell him a mile away!"

The dimorphodon scattered as the giant reptile landed on top of their carriage – and squashed it flat!

Shazz screeched in outrage. "How dare you enter my palace unannounced!"

The newcomer smiled slyly. "Just checking out my new home," he said. "Hmm. Needs some decorating."

"New home?" Teggs stamped over to face him. "But this is the Palace of Perches! The High Flapper lives here!"

"Exactly. And once I've won the Trials, I will *be* the High Flapper, won't

I?" He threw back his beak and laughed. "My name's Grandum. I was enjoying the racing on Morass Minor when I heard the Long Squawk. Thanks for the tip-off, darling – I came at once!"

Arx bustled forwards crossly. "You can't call the High Flapper 'darling'!"

"Can't I?" Grandum frowned. "How about 'Bootface'?"

"Bootface!" Shazz squawked in horror.

"You're the rudest reptile I ever met!" stormed Gipsy.

"Don't get your scales in a skid, sweetheart!" said Grandum. "I bite the tails off ugly dinosaurs like you and eat them for breakfast!"

"You are nasty and rough!" Shazz

declared. "Not fit to be High Flapper!"

"We'll see about that." His saucer-eyes were agleam. "I'll take on anyone in the Trials. Anyone!"

Teggs raised his tail in warning. "I think you should leave, Grandum. Now."

"Fine! You lot are boring me stiff, anyway!" He unfurled his enormous hairy wings. "But I'll tell you this. Once I'm in charge, there will be a lot of changes round here. None of this nicey-nicey rubbish. Everyone will do exactly what I say . . . or else!"

With that, and a very rude noise, he took off – leaving only a nasty whiff in his wake.

"You rotten, stinky devil!" cried

Shazz. She jumped off her cushion and beat her mighty wings as hard and as fast as she could – but it was no good. She couldn't fly a millimetre.

Exhausted, she flopped to the floor while her servants fetched water and fish and fresh crunchy bugs to revive her. "Oh dear!" she sighed. "What am I to do?"

"I think you should cancel the Trials," said Teggs. "At least until things are back to normal."

"I can only do that if the people all agree," said Shazz. "I had better call a Meeting of the Flock for tomorrow, so I can explain it to them."

Arx watched with interest as she crossed to a strange device that stood by a window. It was a cross between a long glass beak and a telescope, with a big red switch on the side. "That looks like a high-speed sound-o-scope," he said. "Is that how you made the Long Squawk?"

"Yes. It sends my voice all over the planet, even into outer space," said Shazz. She cleared her throat, turned on the sound-o-scope, and began to screech and cluck and whistle to her people.

"She's doing the right thing," said Gipsy. "I'm sure no one will mind if the contest is cancelled."

"I can think of someone who will mind a lot," said Arx. "Grandum!"

Teggs said nothing. He was looking worriedly up at the sky. It was empty except for more storm clouds, gathering overhead.

Chapter Four

THE MEETING OF THE FLOCK

The astrosaurs spent the night in the Palace of Perches, as Shazz's guests of honour. They were each given a solid gold perch. The dimorphodon and the alarm pterosaur were delighted, although the others were a bit worried about rolling off in their sleep.

As it turned out, Teggs couldn't sleep anyway.

The mystery of the forgetful flappers was bothering him too much.

As the dawn broke through the window overhead, he could see the sky was even cloudier this morning.

"Funny," Teggs thought. "That cloud looks just like one I saw last night . . . "

Yawning, he decided to find something to eat. He trotted up a steep stone staircase, and soon found a set of doors painted bright red.

"I wonder if this is the larder?" thought Teggs.

It wasn't.

He emerged onto a big balcony. It must have been a mile above the ground. And gathered in the square before him were thousands of grounded pterosaurs – all breeds and shapes and sizes, squashed up in silence together as far as the eye could see. Short little sordes, quirky quetzalcoatlus, wriggling rhamphorhynchus . . .

As soon as they saw Teggs, they squawked and threw little silvery missiles at him. The whole palace shook with the sound of their screeching. Moments later he was half-buried beneath about a billion slimy fish!

"Leave off!" spluttered Teggs. "I'm a vegetarian!"

Then Shazz came up behind him. "What are *you* doing here?" she asked in surprise.

"Look out!" cried Teggs, as more fish rained down. "We're under attack!"

"We most certainly aren't!" she said, snaffling some mackerel with her long beak. "This is how my people greet their High Flapper at a Meeting of the Flock – with a squawk of salute and the gift of fish! You've spoiled my big entrance!"

"Sorry," he murmured sheepishly, skidding on skipjacks to the back of the balcony.

Shazz climbed up the fish pile to greet her people. "Welcome, my flock," she called. "I know it was hard for many of you to get here without working wings."

There were bitter coos and clucks of agreement from the crowd.

"Is there *anyone* here who can fly?" asked Shazz.

Not a single wing was raised.

She sighed. "In that case, I say we postpone the High Flapper Trials until everyone is better and flying high again."

"And what if you *never* get better?" boomed a voice from above.

A gasp went up from the crowd. Teggs narrowed his eyes.

It was Grandum.

"She's tricking you!" cried the hairy, smelly pterosaur. "Shazz doesn't *want* you to fly! She wants to be High Flapper for ever!"

"That's not true!" bellowed Teggs.

"What do *you* know about it, *dinosaur?*" jeered Grandum. He turned back to the crowds. "*I* can fly! Nothing can stop me! Let the Trials go ahead – I'll compete against anyone! And if I'm made High Flapper, I'll show all of you how to fly again . . . which is more than Shazz can do!"

Eager whispers rustled through the crowd.

"We want to fly!" someone called.

"It's easy when you know how!" Grandum told them. "And I do!"

"This pterosaur is nasty and mean!" Shazz cried. "He will make you his slaves!"

"Rubbish," said Grandum. "She's lying. She knows I'm best and she can't stand it!"

"Let the Trials go ahead!" someone shouted. And soon, a ragged chant started up. It grew louder and louder: "*We want the trials! We want the trials!*"

Grandum chuckled. "Well, Bootface?"

Teggs stared at Shazz helplessly.

She lowered her head in defeat. "If the people wish it . . . the Trials must take place!"

The crowds clapped and whooped once more. But now it was Grandum they were cheering. He had sneakily won over the frightened crowd. Teggs scowled as he watched the enormous reptile do a victory dance in mid-air.

He could feel it in his bones . . . in the tiniest dimples of his tail spikes . . . There was more to Grandum than met the eye.

As the cheering went on, Teggs gently led Shazz back into the palace where the other astrosaurs were waiting.

"We heard everything," said Gipsy. Her head-crest had flushed purple with gloom.

"*Someone's* got to stand up to Grandum," Iggy declared. "But who?"

"What about Sprite?" Arx suggested.

"He's a gutsy little guy," Teggs agreed. "I'd be sad to lose him from the *Sauropod* if he won, but . . . "

He tailed off. Sprite squawked as he led the dimorphodon down the steps. They all looked miserable, with puffy eyes and runny beaks.

"Oh no!" cried Shazz. "Even *they* have forgotten how to fly!"

Iggy stared at the dimorphodon. "Lads, what happened? You were fine yesterday!"

The whole flock shrugged helplessly.

"What about the alarm pterosaur?" asked Teggs.

At the sound of her name she appeared heroically at the top of the steps. She launched herself into the air and flew gracefully for a few moments . . . then fell like a brick. Teggs winced as she landed rather painfully on one of Arx's horns.

"You poor thing," said Gipsy kindly, lifting her free. "Go and have a lie down."

"Lie down," she agreed. "*Squaaawk!*" And she waddled stiffly away.

"It's hopeless," sighed Iggy. "If only *you* could fly, Captain. You'd soon sort out that grotty Grandum."

"Me?" Teggs stared at him. "Iggy, you're a genius!"

Iggy blinked. "I am?"

Teggs nodded, grinning. "We've got just one tiny chance of stopping whatever Grandum's up to. But  we'll have to work fast and we'll have to work hard. Are you with me?"

Gipsy, Arx and Iggy proudly saluted. "As always!"

And so Teggs explained what they needed to do . . .

Chapter Five

THE TRIALS BEGIN

One week later, pterosaurs from all over Squawk Major gathered on Beak Mountain to watch the High Flapper Trials. Normally they would simply fly to the summit and watch from one of the many million perches. Now they had to walk, or cycle, or hang-glide from the nearest hills. It took them quite a long time.

But most pterosaurs decided to stay at home. What was the point of going to watch?

Grandum was the only one taking part!

Chief Judge Floss was in charge of the Trials. He was an elderly quetzalcoatlus with grey, leathery skin. He had helped to choose *twelve* High Flappers in his long life, and Shazz had been the greatest of all. He sighed. Grandum was not his idea of a good replacement.

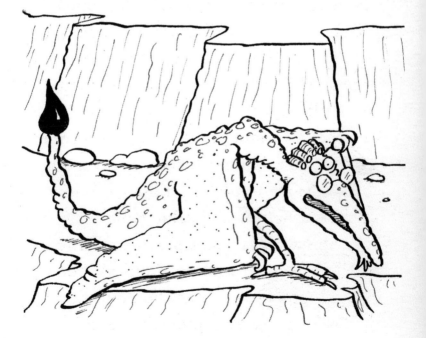

The huge, smelly pterosaur was grinning like a gargoyle beside the winner's podium. "Why are we waiting?"

"The Trials will begin as soon as Lady Shazz arrives," said Floss.

"She's probably too busy blubbing in her palace 'cause she knows I'm best," laughed Grandum. "Tell you what, grandpa – why don't you just make me High Flapper now? No one else is coming!"

"*Someone* is!" gasped a voice in the crowd. "Look!"

"Someone else can fly!" cried another. "They are flying this way! And they're bringing . . . the High Flapper!"

Floss looked up in wonder. Grandum looked up in fury.

A funny-looking flying reptile was sweeping towards the summit of Beak Mountain. It was about the size of a stegosaurus, and covered in red

feathers. Its wingspan was the length of a double-decker bus. Shazz dangled proudly in its enormous claws.

"This is my champion!" Shazz declared as the newcomer gently set her down beside the judges. "He has come to enter the Trials!"

"My name is Flappo the Fearless!" boomed the big red pterosaur. The flocking crowds cheered and clapped.

Floss smiled at Grandum. "Looks like you have competition after all!"

"I'm not scared," sneered Grandum. "I'll squish him! Squash him! Marmalize and mash him!"

"This isn't a wrestling match!" said Floss sternly. "These are trials of skill."

"Then I'll squish him skilfully!" Grandum cried.

"Let's just get on with it," said Flappo. "Before you bore everyone to death!"

The crowd laughed and clapped their

wings. Grandum's eyes
narrowed. He was sure
he'd seen this Flappo
character somewhere
before . . .

And he had.

What Grandum didn't know – what
nobody knew – was that Flappo the
Fearless didn't exist.

It was Teggs in disguise!

Teggs didn't like tricking people, and
he hated cheats. But he wasn't doing
this to help himself. He had to save the
people of Squawk Major from a
wicked would-be ruler.

All the astrosaurs had been very busy
over the last week. Gipsy had designed
a special flying costume for Teggs, and
the dimorphodon had stitched it
together. The wings were mechanical
and remote-controlled, built by Iggy
and hidden by feathers. Thanks to a
special camera in the beak, Iggy could

see everything Teggs could — which allowed the clever iguanodon to steer his captain through the skies with ease. There was also a two-way radio so they could keep in touch — along with one or two other useful gadgets . . .

Meanwhile, Arx had been running special tests on lots of pterosaurs who had forgotten how to fly. Teggs had hoped that if a cure could be found, he might not need to take part in the Trials at all. But it wasn't so simple.

"I can't see a thing wrong with any of these people," Arx had sighed, the night before the Trials. "They *should* be able to fly. The problem isn't in their wings — it's in their heads!"

Now Teggs looked sadly round at the crowd. He hoped Arx could solve that problem soon. And he hoped no one found out he was really an astrosaur in a pterosaur suit. That would get him disqualified at once!

Floss took his place between his junior judges, Moss and Joss. "Let the Trials commence!" he cried.

The crowds cheered and clapped, happy to be distracted from their woes for a while.

"The first Trial is the Trial of Squawking," Floss went on. "From one mile high you must give your best squawk. You will be marked on loudness, pitch and overall quality. Good luck!"

Grandum went first. With a rude noise and a smelly pong he burst into flight. Soon he was only a speck in the cloudy sky.

"Hoooooooooo— arrrrrrrrrrrrrrrrrhhhhhhhhhhhh- wuurrrrrrrrrrk!" came an echoing squawk from on high. It was loud and clear and pleasing to the ear. The crowd clapped with enthusiasm.

"Beat that, fatso!" said Grandum rudely as he flapped back down to earth.

Teggs simply raised his front legs and hoped Iggy was ready at the remote control. His wings flapped a couple of times, then he felt himself lifting up into the sky. His flight was a bit wobbly, since he and Iggy hadn't had much time to practise. But no one seemed to notice as he hurtled up towards the clouds.

"Can you hear me, Captain?" said

Gipsy over the two-way radio.

Teggs looked down at the dizzying view of the mountain far below, and quickly wished he hadn't. "Loud and clear."

"Switch on your loudspeaker," she said.

Teggs flicked a switch hidden in his false beak, and heard Gipsy take a deep breath. Long ago, in the wild, hadrosaurs used their hollow head-crests to boost their voices when calling to their herds. It was a trick they could still use today.

"Arrooooooooooo—
aaaaaaaaaaaahhhhhhhhh—grrrrrrrruk-
ooooooooh!"

Gipsy's amplified hoot was incredible. It nearly took Teggs's ears off. The sound echoed for miles and miles. It even started an avalanche on another mountain nearby.

Chuckling to himself, Teggs was steered back down to the summit, where the crowds were applauding wildly. Grandum was fuming with rage.

Floss conferred with Moss and Joss. "And the results are . . . Grandum: seven points. Flappo: *nine* points!"

Again, the audience burst into excited applause. Grandum pretended to clap, like a good loser – though he was clearly furious. "You won't be leading for long," he hissed. "It's the Trial of Acrobatics next, and I am *hot!*"

"Is that why you're so smelly?" Teggs asked innocently. But as the Trial began, his tummy was doing acrobatics of its own. Could Iggy match Grandum's skill by remote control?

Grandum took off with another rude noise and instantly looped the loop. The crowds clapped and gasped as he spun and spiralled over their heads like a big, hairy boomerang. He flew straight up in the air like a rocket, then did seventeen somersaults on his way back down to the summit. The crowd happily squawked their approval.

"You see, Flappo? These fools love me," sneered Grandum, panting for breath. "I'll soon have them all in my power – and you too!"

"We'll see about that," said Teggs.

First, he took off *backwards*! Then he did a flapping flip in mid air and performed a double loop-the-loop. The crowd went crazy as he zigzagged through the sky, flying higher and higher.

Iggy chortled over the earpiece. "These mechanical wings handle like a dream!"

"More like a nightmare to me," groaned Teggs as his flying suit sent him through *twenty* perfect somersaults. "I feel air-sick!"

At last he started to spiral stylishly back down to the mountain-top, before landing as light as a feather.

The crowd's applause almost started another avalanche.

"Grandum scores eight points," Floss declared. "But Flappo scores *nine* points!"

"Bravo, my champion," called Shazz over the happy squawking of the great flock. "Now, let's break for lunch!"

But Grandum poked his beak in Teggs's ear. "Think you're clever, don't you?" he hissed. "Well, no one makes a fool out of me, Flappo! You're going to find the rest of the Trials a lot tougher. Just you wait!"

Chapter Six

RIDDLES, RIDDLES, RIDDLES

Teggs was dismayed to find that lunch was a fish and woodlouse salad. As he picked out the fish and woodlice and tried to suck lettuce up his false beak, he noticed Grandum wasn't eating. Instead the big bully was talking to a pair of shifty-looking woolly mammoths.

"What are mammoths doing here?" he wondered.

"Grandum came here from Morass Minor, home of the mammoth Space-Car Races," Iggy reminded him over the radio. "He must have brought some friends with him to cheer him on."

"I suppose so," said Teggs. When Grandum saw his enemy watching, he and the mammoths moved off into a nearby cave.

Once the food was finished, Teggs flapped over to meet Iggy and Gipsy in Shazz's royal carriage further down the mountain. This was their only chance to make any repairs to his flying suit. The two astrosaurs grinned and cheered as their captain came inside.

"How does it feel to be a top-class pterosaur?" asked Gipsy.

"Give me four legs on the ground anyday!" Teggs felt hot, sick and sweaty in his suit of feathers. "No offence, Sprite!"

The dimorphodon cheeped and saluted. He was sitting in the corner building his own set of robotic wings. "He's making new wings for *all* the dimorphodon,"

Iggy explained. "They'll do anything to fly again!"

"They may be small, but they're plucky!" said Teggs fondly. Then he sighed. "You know, beating Grandum is only half the battle. We have to beat whatever is ailing the pterosaurs too. Any word from Arx?"

"Not yet," said Iggy, oiling Teggs's wings. "He's still hard at work back at the palace."

"I'm sure we'll hear something soon," said Gipsy, sewing up a small tear in the suit. "Now, it's the Trial of Riddles next. Good luck!"

"I'll need it," Teggs groaned. "I'm rubbish at riddles! Grandum was right, I *will* find the next Trials harder!"

"He was just trying to scare you," said Iggy.

But Teggs couldn't help thinking there was more to it than that.

Teggs was soon back at the summit. He landed next to Shazz.

"Hello, *Flappo*," she said with a wink.

"You haven't seen Chief Judge Floss anywhere, have you? Moss and Joss can't find him."

"There he is," said Teggs, pointing. "With Grandum and that mammoth!"

Shazz turned up her royal beak. "Why would he want to talk to *them*? And how come he's suddenly got so much fatter?"

"He must have really enjoyed his lunch," said Teggs enviously.

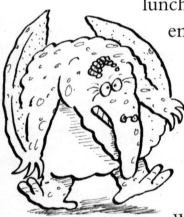

"He doesn't *look* like he enjoyed it," said Shazz. "His face has gone all wrinkly. It almost looks as if he's wearing a mask!"

"Right," said Floss gruffly, plonking his portly body down beside Joss and Moss. "Contestants, take your places on the puzzle perches."

The puzzle perches were each carved in the shape of a question mark.

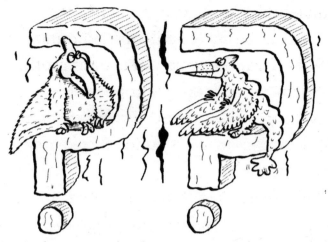

Grandum perched on one, Teggs on the other.

"Right, then. Riddles. Here we go." Floss picked up the question card. "Flappo – what can't you see but is always ahead of you?"

Teggs mind went blank. "Er . . ."

Then Gipsy hissed over the radio: "The future!"

Teggs grinned. Of course! "The *future* is always ahead of you, though you can't see it!"

The crowd clapped politely.

"How dreary!" yawned Grandum. "The proper answer is — *an invisible narg*. You can't see an invisible narg but it's always ahead of you."

"It is not!" Teggs protested.

"Prove it!" chuckled Grandum. Even Chief Judge Floss roared with laughter. "An invisible narg is the correct answer!"

Joss turned to Floss. "What *is* an invisible narg, anyway?"

"If you don't know *that*, you shouldn't be sitting here at all," said Floss sniffily. "One point to Grandum. Nothing at all for Flappo."

"But that's not fair!" cried Joss.

"It's an outrage!" added Moss.

"Who is the Chief Judge around

here?" said Floss, with a menacing glint in his eyes.

Teggs's feathers bristled. He knew that his answer was right. What was Floss playing at?

"Next riddle," bellowed Floss. "Flappo, if you were pushed downstairs, what would you fall against?"

Teggs shut his eyes and tried to think. Grandum started humming smugly like he knew the answer.

"I know!" cried Teggs. "If you were pushed downstairs, you'd fall against *your will*!"

Again, the audience clapped and cheered.

But Grandum shook his head. "I think you'll find the *real* answer is that you'd fall against your big feathery bottom!"

A great gasp went up from the crowd.

"Correct!" cried Floss.

An even greater gasp went up.

Shazz gave him a hard stare. "Are you feeling OK?"

"Never better," Floss chuckled. "Two points to Grandum. Nothing to Flappo!"

"Er, surely Flappo deserves at least *half* a point?" Joss protested.

"His answer was very clever," said Moss.

"Softies," Floss snarled. "He can have a *quarter* of a point! Nothing more!"

Teggs's beak flapped open in disbelief. A wave of startled clucks and squawks went through the crowd. Nothing like this had ever been seen at a Trial before.

But Grandum was cool and calm, relaxing on his perch like a pterosaur whose troubles were over . . .

Back at the palace, Arx was taking a walk in the gardens to clear his head. He had been thinking so hard his horns were aching. He had tested the pterosaurs till he was blue in the face. But he simply couldn't figure it out. How could flying reptiles forget how to fly in a matter of moments? Why so many all at once – even members of the *Sauropod* crew? And how come none of them could learn how to fly again, except Grandum?

He glanced up at the sky. That was another thing – how come the clouds never seemed to move here on Squawk Major?

Despairing, he paused beside a royal pool. Fish were darting through the clear blue water, their scales glinting and glittering. Arx stared at the whirling patterns they made. The way they moved was almost hypnotic . . .

He blinked.

Hypnotic?

"That's it!" he yelled, and the fish scattered. "Someone has *hypnotized* the people into forgetting how to fly! One by one they've all fallen under a spell. That's why lessons made no difference!" He clapped his heavy feet together, then frowned. "But how could anyone hypnotize an entire planet?"

And an awful thought struck him.

Shazz used a high-speed sound-o-scope to send messages around the planet or out into space. What if someone was using a similar device to send a hypnotic signal all  over Squawk Major? A signal that was too high to be heard but which went to work directly on the brain — convincing the people of Squawk Major that they could not fly, even though they really could.

A *hypno-beam*!

Almost hoping he was wrong, Arx rushed back inside the palace to the sound-o-scope. It was the work of minutes to reverse the settings so it could *receive* signals. And by boosting the sound frequencies he could hear any secret messages.

Soon he heard a quiet, sinister voice broadcasting over and over: ". . . forget how to fly . . . You will forget how to fly . . . You will forget . . ."

Arx nodded grimly. He didn't know where the hypno-beam was coming from. He didn't know how he could stop it. But one thing he *did* know – the voice sounded a lot like Grandum's.

Chapter Seven

HEAD IN THE CLOUDS

Back at the Trials, Teggs was finding it hard going. Whatever he did, however good he was, however much the crowd cheered him on – Chief Judge Floss would always rule against him!

"He wasn't like this before lunch," Teggs grumbled to himself. "It's like he's become a completely different person!"

In the Trial of Swiftness, Teggs beat Grandum in the two thousand metre flying race by two seconds. But Grandum complained the wind had been blowing against him – so Floss gave him an extra point!

In the Trial of Nimbleness, Teggs dodged fifty heat-seeking flying fish thanks to Iggy's super-cool steering. Grandum only dodged *two* before Floss ruled he was clearly the best and gave him *three* extra points!

Worst of all was the Trial of Judgement. Both contestants listened to an argument between two pterodactyls who wanted to fish in the same pond. Teggs thought they should share the spot and take it in turns to go fishing – Joss and Moss gave him two points each. But Grandum said he would blow up the pond so nobody could fish there, to teach them both a lesson. Floss gave him *five* points!

Now they had come to the final test. This was the Trial of Stamina — a hundred-mile flight across the sea and back. Teggs balanced nervously on the starting perch. He was two points behind. But if he won this race the crowd would see he was the overall champion, whatever Floss might say.

"Captain," hissed Iggy through the earpiece. "I don't know if my remote control has enough range for this test. You might go out of control! You might fall and splash into the sea!"

"It's a chance I'll have to take," said Teggs. "We can't give up now!"

Then Gipsy spoke. "Captain! I've just heard from Arx. He knows what's stopping the people from flying. It's a hypno-beam!"

"Of course!" hissed Teggs. "Where is it coming from?"

"He's working that out now. But he thinks Grandum could be behind it."

Teggs glared across at Grandum. "That would explain why *he* can still fly when nobody else can. Not unless they've got robotic wings like me, anyway!"

"Let the Trial begin!" yelled Chief Judge Floss.

Teggs tensed himself for action.

"On your marks – get set – *go*!"

Grandum was away first. Teggs choked on a blast of smelly air from the pterosaur's backside, but soon caught up.

They flew over a range of snow-topped mountains, and out across the sea. It was colder here, and Teggs was glad of his feathers. The grey clouds were blotting out the sun. In fact they hid the whole orange sky from view.

The miles passed by. Slowly, surely, Grandum was pulling ahead.

"Faster, Iggy!" Teggs hissed.

"Sorry, Captain," said Iggy in his ear. "I'm pushing you as fast as I can!"

"Then I'll just have to try surprise tactics," Teggs decided. "Hey, Grandum! The astrosaurs are on to you! They know about your hypno-beam!"

Grandum squawked and spun round in mid-air. "What? No! Impossible!"

"It's true!" Teggs soared past him with a smile. "They will track it down and destroy it. Then everyone will be able to fly again, wherever and whenever they want!"

"They won't!" snarled Grandum. "I won't *let* them – because *I'll* be High Flapper, not you!"

And suddenly, he swooped down and attacked Teggs!

Teggs gasped as Grandum grabbed hold of his feathered tail and shook

him around. He fought back, pecking
Grandum with his false beak.

"Watch those wings, Captain!" hissed
Iggy. "If anything happens to them,
you'll fall!"

Teggs wriggled free of Grandum's
grip. Iggy steered him straight upwards.
"You can hide up here in the clouds,"
he explained. "When Grandum comes
looking, we'll surprise him!"

But it was Teggs who got the
surprise.

He didn't fly
through the clouds.
He bounced *off*
them, head first
– *Klang!*

"Metal clouds?"
thought Teggs
dizzily. The world
whirled around
him. His hidden camera, squashed flat
by the impact, slipped out of his suit.
His brain seemed to rattle in his head
like an acorn in a drum.

"I see you've stumbled upon our little
secret." Grandum laughed nastily. "Or
rather, you've flown straight *into* it!"

Teggs could feel himself passing out.
But before his eyes fell shut he saw a
big, dark hole open up in the clouds
above him . . . and he smelled
Grandum's foul breath as the pterosaur
pushed him inside.

Chapter Eight

THE MAMMOTH MASTERPLAN

Back in the royal carriage, Iggy and Gipsy were very worried. They'd been watching their captain's struggles on a small screen. But now it was blank.

Iggy spoke urgently into the two-way radio. "Calling Captain Teggs! Can you hear me?"

Silence.

"It's no good," he sighed. "His radio must be broken. Either that, or . . ."

"Something terrible happened when he flew into those clouds!" Gipsy gave a hoot of alarm. "We have to find him! But how?"

Sprite looked up from his robotic wings and chirruped.

Gipsy stared at him. Then she smiled. "That's a wild idea . . . but it could be our only chance!"

Teggs woke up in a very strange place.

It looked like a kind of construction site – but all the builders were woolly mammoths! There were loads of them, drilling and digging, sawing and sanding,

leaning on sledgehammers or slurping from great big mugs of tea.

"Gipsy?" he whispered into his radio. "Iggy? Is anyone there?"

But there was no reply.

Another mammoth stomped past close by. He was using his curvy tusks like a screwdriver, putting together some metal rails. In the distance Teggs could see a huge helter-skelter, a ghost train, some swing-boats – and realized that the mammoths beside him were building a rollercoaster! But where in the world was he?

Then he realized he was lying on thick, grey cotton wool. Above him, more clouds were scudding across an expanse of burnt orange.

"I'm up in the sky!" he gasped.

"Who's a clever Flappo, then!" sneered Grandum, looking up from a set of building plans. "That's why we had to stop every pterosaur from flying. So we could build up here in peace!" He scowled. "Our hypno-beam should have worked on everyone. How come you're still flapping about?"

"Perhaps you're not as smart as you think," said Teggs. "Tell me, where *is* this hypno-beam of yours?"

"Nowhere you can get at it," Grandum guffawed. "It's in an empty spaceship, orbiting the planet."

"And the clouds we saw gathering are fakes," Teggs realized. "From down below they look fluffy" He jumped up and down, testing their strength. "But they're really as solid as stone!"

Grandum nodded proudly. "The cloud barrier keeps my building work hidden from prying eyes."

"But just what *are* you building?" Teggs demanded.

"What do you think? A *mammoth* funfair!" Grandum laughed. "Me and the boys, we own the Space-Car Races on Morass Minor. Now we're expanding into theme parks. And since there's no room left on Morass Minor, we're building one on the planet next door instead – right here!"

"But you have no right to build anything on Squawk Major!" said Teggs. "This is not your world!"

"It *will* be, when I become High Flapper!" Grandum grinned. "I'll make sure its people stay flightless forever. The only things in the sky will be my brilliant, noisy, stinky funfair rides, the biggest in the universe. One day, they will stretch right round the planet!"

Teggs glared at him. "I suppose that's the good thing about building in the skies, isn't it? With this cloud barrier to hide you, no one will know what you're up to – until it's too late!"

"Correct." Grandum grinned. "It will also make my funfair *much* easier to keep clean. Every day, a million tourists will turn up, eating and drinking and pooing all over the place. So at night, we'll simply dump all the rubbish over the sides onto the planet below!"

"That's monstrous!" shouted Teggs. "Those poor pterosaurs – like caged canaries, trying to dodge the muck you throw down from above!"

"'Those poor pterosaurs'? You make it sound like you're not one of them." Grandum looked at him suspiciously. "Hey! Your feathers are falling out!"

Teggs gulped. His costume had been torn in the fight with Grandum, and red feathers were littered all around him. A little one caught in his nose and made him sneeze.

"*Aaaaaa-Chooooooo!*"

He sneezed so hard that his false beak fell off!

The mammoths round him gasped. But Grandum only smiled nastily. "So! No wonder the hypno-beam didn't work on you! 'Flappo the Fearless' is only Shazz's pet dinosaur in a suit!"

"My name is Captain Teggs," he replied. "I'm an *astro*saur in a suit! And that means *you* are in big trouble."

Grandum shook his head. "Not when you are in my hidden cloud base, cut off from all your friends!"

Teggs saw twenty ugly mammoths closing in on him. "Ah. You may have a point."

"I brought you here to get you out of the way," said Grandum. "Now no one can stop me becoming High Flapper! I'll tell the judges you got tired and fell in the ocean."

Teggs scoffed. "They'll never believe a story like that!"

"Chief Judge Floss will." Grandum's eyes were gleaming. "Or rather, my mammoth friend who's *pretending* to be Chief Judge Floss will!"

"Of course!" groaned Teggs. "No

wonder Floss suddenly looked and sounded so different. And no wonder he's been giving you points you don't deserve. He's a miserable mammoth in disguise!"

"We had a special Floss costume made, just in case of trouble," said Grandum smugly. "The *real* Chief Judge has been our prisoner since lunch time!"

Teggs glared at him. "You rotten cheats."

"Look who's talking!" cried Grandum. "But don't worry, Teggs. The truth about you will never come out ... because you will never escape our clutches!"

Teggs tried to run, but the mammoths were all around him. He swiped at one with his tail, but his Flappo disguise was so heavy and bulky, he couldn't fight very well. Big feet stomped and kicked him. Long tusks poked him. Twenty sweaty trunks held him down.

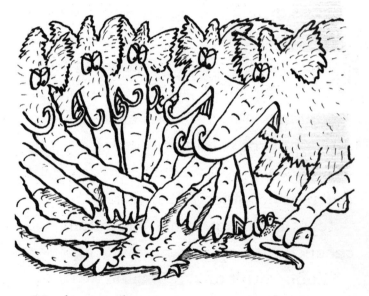

He knew there was no way out . . .

Chapter Nine

BATTLE IN THE SKY!

Teggs stared furiously at Grandum. "What are you going to do to me?"

Grandum chuckled. "I'm going to melt you down in a vat of molten metal, you dismal dinosaur! You'll end up as part of a bumper car, or a candyfloss machine, or a bit of rickety rollercoaster track . . . "

The mammoths picked Teggs up and dragged him away, struggling for his life. The vat of molten metal was close by, oily and bubbling. Its heat seared his scaly skin.

"Sorry I can't stay to watch," Grandum shouted. "I've got to finish

checking some plans – and then I've got a race to win."

"My crew will stop you," Teggs told him. "You'll never succeed!"

"We'll see," said Grandum. "Goodbye, Teggs! Goodbye forever!"

Teggs heard him flap away.

"We'll throw in the dinosaur on the count of three, boys," said a very big mammoth.

"I can't count up to three!" his friend complained.

The big mammoth sighed. "All right then, on the count of *two*."

"Is that the one after four?" asked another.

"No, one is after zero!"

"Shall we throw him in on the count of zero, then?"

"Shut up!"

Teggs listened to them squabble. Slowly, he was gathering his strength.

"Look, we won't use numbers, OK?" said the big mammoth. "We'll use letters instead. When we get up to C, we'll throw him in."

A short mammoth scratched his head. "You want us to throw him in the sea?"

"I mean the *letter* C! Now come on. A – B—"

"A bee?" cried the short one. "What bee? Where?"

"A bee! Help, a bee's coming to sting

us!" cried the mammoths.

And while they were panicking, Teggs burst into action.

First, he flapped his robotic wings and scratched the mammoths beside him with his plastic claws.

"We've been stung!" they wailed. "Help!"

Then he flexed his muscles and ripped right through his costume. "Now I've got room to move!" cried Teggs.

He swung his tail with all his strength, and smashed the big mammoth into a half-finished rollercoaster – the whole lot came crashing down. Two more came to get him, trumpeting in fury, but he tripped them up and trod on their trunks.

"There are no bees!" the small mammoth shouted. "Get him!"

Teggs gritted his teeth. The spikes on his back flushed red and he raised his tail. He would show these mammoths what an astrosaur was made of!

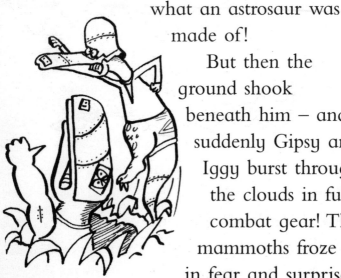

But then the ground shook beneath him – and suddenly Gipsy and Iggy burst through the clouds in full combat gear! The mammoths froze in fear and surprise.

"Guys!" Teggs beamed. "How did *you* get up here?"

"We hitched a lift!", said Gipsy.

And a moment later, fifty daring dimorphodon with robotic wings came flapping inside. Just behind them was the alarm pterosaur in a hang-glider.

Teggs laughed with joy. "Come on, crew! Let's show these mangy mammoths what a team of astrosaurs can do!"

They leaped into action! Iggy's stun-claws sparked and flashed. Gipsy's high-kicks and snout-jabs found their mark. Teggs's tail sliced through the air like a battle-axe. The dimorphodon dive-bombed from above, and the alarm pterosaur squawked at full blast in the mammoths' big hairy ears.

Soon, not one of their foes was left standing.

"Nice work," said Teggs, catching his breath. "But we've got to stop Grandum! You won't believe what he's planning!"

"We will," Iggy assured him. "We heard every word! Your broken radio couldn't *receive* messages, but it still transmitted them!"

"Phew!" sighed Teggs. "Then you know Grandum's hypno-beam is up in orbit?"

Gipsy nodded. "We told Arx. Don't worry, he's on the case!"

Back in the Palace of Perches, Arx looked up from his gadgets with a whoop of joy. "I've found it!" He called the *Sauropod* on his communicator, his horns quivering with excitement.

"This is First Officer Arx. The spaceship carrying the hypno-beam is in sector B-two! Can you locate it?"

"Just looking now," rumbled Alass, the ankylosaurus left in charge. Arx heard her flick some switches. "Aha! Spaceship located!"

"Launch dung torpedoes," cried Arx. "I want it blasted out of the sky!"

"Leave it to me!" said Alass. "Launching torpedoes . . . *now*!"

Arx could hear the distant crump of a huge and very smelly explosion.

"Direct hit!" Alass reported. "We've blasted it right out of the sky, sir, just as you asked. It's on its way down to the planet."

Arx gasped. "But . . . out of the sky

was a figure of speech! I didn't *mean* it!"

"Oh. Sorry sir," said Alass. "But I'm afraid it's going to fall on Squawk Major in just a few minutes!"

"No, it won't," Arx realized. "If it's falling from sector B-two, it'll crash into the mammoths' fake clouds!"

Alass breathed a sigh of relief. "That's all right then!"

"It isn't!" yelled Arx. "Teggs is up there – with Iggy and Gipsy and everyone else!"

Back above the clouds, Teggs and the others were looking for Grandum.

"I hope he hasn't flown off already," said Teggs, as they peeped about from behind a helter-skelter. "Now I've broken my Flappo-suit I can't go after him!"

"No, look!" hooted Gipsy. "There he is!"

Grandum was looking at some funfair blueprints held up by a pair of mammoths.

The alarm pterosaur gave a fierce squawk and launched herself towards him on her hang-glider. She flew right through the blueprints! Grandum gave a cry of alarm.

Teggs smiled grimly. "And those aren't the *only* plans of yours we'll be ruining!"

Grandum gasped. "You!"

"Hope you don't mind, but I've brought a few of my crew along," Teggs said.

Gipsy nodded proudly. "And we're going to bring your high-flying dreams crashing down to earth!"

Never was a truer word spoken.

For at that very moment, the empty spaceship with the hypno-beam on board came whistling down from above like a giant, dung-splattered bullet – heading straight for the middle of the funfair!

"Look out!" Teggs shouted. He and his friends dived for cover behind a big dipper.

The spaceship exploded in a massive ball of flame. The blast wrecked every ride for miles around. The only things still standing were a bit of rollercoaster, half a big wheel and a coconut shy.

Grandum snapped his beak in seething rage. "You have destroyed the hypno-beam – now those pesky pterosaurs will be able to fly again! And just look at my fabulous funfair –

it's ruined!" He fixed the astrosaurs
with a terrible stare. "You'll pay for this
– with your lives!"

Dozens of mammoth builders, all
sooty, singed and scorched, closed in on
Teggs and his crew at Grandum's
command. But then the ground started
to shake. A huge hole opened
up in the clouds right by
Iggy's feet. He yelped
and jumped aside
– and almost fell
through *another* hole.

Gipsy gasped as a
huge split appeared in
the clouds beneath her,
revealing the snowy mountains
below. "What's happening?" she yelled.

"The crashing spaceship has
weakened the cloud barrier!" cried
Teggs. "That's the only thing holding us
up! If it collapses now, this whole place
will fall apart!"

"I'm off!" said Grandum.

"Coward!" shouted Teggs. "What about the builders? You can't just leave them behind – you're their boss!"

"Not any more!" he cried. "Mammoths – you're sacked. Happy landings!"

Grandum dived for a gap in the clouds.

"Oh no you don't!" said Teggs, leaping after him.

352

He landed on the shaggy pterosaur's back. The next thing he knew they were tumbling through the air together.

"Get off me, you fool!" gasped Grandum.

Teggs clung on. "Not a chance!"

"But I can't flap my wings. You'll make us crash!"

"Down we go together!" shouted Teggs, shutting his eyes as they fell faster and faster . . .

Chapter Ten

A FLAPPY ENDING?

Back on Beak Mountain, the echoes of the explosion rumbled like endless thunder. The flock squawked and clattered in alarm. Shazz looked up, her beady eyes full of worry. It sounded like the sky was about to fall in.

And then it did!

The clouds cracked open and started raining down in chunks all around them. The fake Chief Judge Floss hid under a table, wailing like a big baby.

Shazz unfurled her mighty wings and held them up like long, leathery umbrellas. "Listen to me, all of you!" she yelled. "We may not be able to fly,

but we can still
use our wings –
as shields to
protect our
fellow reptiles!
Open them out
and keep your
heads down! We
shall be safe
then, you'll see!"

Some little
pterosaurs sheltered under her as the
strange lumps of cloud kept raining
down. Tools and timber, even a coconut
or two fell with them. But all the
missiles bounced harmlessly off the
bigger reptiles' tough, protective wings.

Finally, the bombardment stopped.
The thunder ended.

Shazz looked up to see a brilliant
orange sky overhead. The sun was
shining fat and red, warming the
mountain with its light.

A small pterodactyl peeped out from under one of her wings. "We made it!" he cheeped. "Three cheers for the High Flapper, hip-hip—"

"*Squaaaaawk!*" bellowed the thankful flock. They couldn't believe what had just happened.

But things were about to get even stranger.

"Look!" someone cried. "It's Grandum and Flappo! They're coming back!"

"And Flappo's riding on Grandum's back!"

"That's not Flappo – it's a stegosaurus! Where did *he* come from?"

Shazz gasped. "Oh my goodness!"

Teggs was riding Grandum like a jockey on a horse, clinging on to his neck. The big hairy pterosaur's eyes were bulging as he struggled to keep flapping. "Get off me, you idiot!" he snarled.

"And fall to my doom?" Teggs scoffed. "I really *would* be an idiot then, wouldn't I!"

With a thump, a skid and a rude noise, Grandum landed flat on his beak right in front of the judges' table. He lay in a daze, while Teggs beamed at Joss and Moss. They stared at him in shock.

"Sorry to drop in on you like this!"

he said. "I'm Captain Teggs of the DSS *Sauropod*. And this smelly creature is under arrest!"

Suddenly, Chief Judge Floss burst out from beneath the table. "He is not! He landed back here first — so he's the winner of the Trials! Grandum's the new High Flapper!"

A gasp went up from the crowd.

"You're not even a judge!" cried Teggs. He grabbed hold of Floss's crooked beak and yanked it off . . . to reveal the squashed woolly face of a mammoth underneath!

An even bigger gasp went up from the crowd. A lot of the flock fainted.

Joss cleared his throat. "I'm afraid that even if Chief Judge Floss *is* a mammoth, he's still correct. Grandum has won the trials. And no one can put the High Flapper under arrest. He will rule Squawk Major for ten years!"

Shazz's wings drooped.

But Teggs shook his head. "Rubbish! Grandum can't become High Flapper any more than I can!"

"What do you mean?" Shazz cried.

"I realized when I was riding him here," said Teggs. "I could hear his wings whirring and creaking, and the sound of jet rockets firing. Since when did a true pterosaur need mechanical wings and jet rockets to help him fly?" He grabbed hold of Grandum's ear and pulled hard.

Grandum's face stretched and stretched . . . and pinged off like an old rubber glove.

He was a mammoth too!

The loudest gasp ever recorded rang around Beak Mountain. The pterosaurs that had already fainted woke up and promptly fainted again.

"That's why he smelled so bad," Teggs explained. "A big hairy mammoth squashed into a leather suit for days on end – what a *stink*! And every time he took off he let out filthy fumes from his hidden rockets!"

"But why did he do it?" croaked Shazz.

"Because only a pterosaur can be High Flapper, and he wanted control of your world." He smiled. "I think we should let Grandum explain his entire evil plan later – at his own *trial!*"

Shazz gave a commanding squawk. At once, some burly pterosaurs stepped up to guard the mammoths. "But where is the real Floss?"

"He's here!" panted Arx, lumbering

through the crowd
with the old judge
on his back. Floss
looked startled but
unharmed. "I
found him on my
way here, tied up
and guarded by
a mammoth."

"The beastly
things are
everywhere!" Shazz declared, helping
Floss down.

"Well, I dealt with *that* one, anyway,"
grinned Arx, waggling his horns. "He
should be asleep for some time."

"Well done, Arx." Teggs saluted his
first officer. "You saved the day."

"I'm so glad you saved yourself!"
said Arx. "But what about Gipsy and
Iggy and—"

"Look!" shouted Shazz.

Teggs turned to see an incredible

sight. Three big clouds were sailing through the air towards them, each one towed by a straining flock of dimorphodon using their powerful robotic wings. On one cloud, masses of mammoths huddled together for safety. On another, the alarm pterosaur sat perched atop a big pile of funfair scrap metal. And on the other stood Gipsy and Iggy.

"You made it!" Teggs cheered as the dimorphodon came in to land with their extraordinary load.

"This is all that's left of Grandum's wicked scheme," called Iggy.

"So we thought we should tidy it up," Gipsy added. "Now Squawk Major is left lovely and unpolluted, just like before."

"Not quite," sighed Shazz. "We still can't fly."

"But you *can!*" Arx cleared his throat and called to the crowd. "Grandum was using a hypno-beam to make you think you couldn't fly. That beam has been destroyed, so now your minds should be back to normal!"

A breathless hush settled on the mountain. It was the sound of a million pterosaurs holding their breath, hoping this green triceratops was right.

"Well, go on then," Teggs urged them. "Try it!"

Shazz tried first. She gave her wings a nervous flap and rose up in the air. She flapped them again, and rose higher. And higher . . .

"I'm flying!" she cried. "Look! I'm *flying*!"

"So am I!" cried a pterodactyl, rising from the crowd.

"And me!" squawked Floss. "Look at me! I'm shaking my booty!"

Teggs laughed. Soon the air was filled

with flying reptiles, squawking and screeching with joy. The dimorphodon pecked off their mechanical wings and the alarm pterosaur chucked away her hang-glider. They looped the loop round Gipsy and Iggy, and buzzed past Teggs and Arx in a blissful blur.

None of the astrosaurs had seen a sight so wonderful in all their lives.

"Well, Arx," said Teggs. "This planet's problems are solved. Its people can live flappily ever after!"

Arx nodded. "And once a new High Flapper is chosen, Shazz can enjoy a nice long holiday." He paused. "Come to think of it, *we* could use a holiday too!"

"Holiday?" Teggs pulled a face. "Forget it! There's just time for a quick celebration dinner, then it's back to the *Sauropod*." He smiled. "Even over all that squawking, I can hear the call of another adventure! Can't you?"

THE END

TALKING DINOSAUR!

How to say the dinosaur and pterosaur names in this book . . .

ANKYLOSAUR –
an-KI-*loh*-SORE

STYGIMOLOCH –
STIJ-*i*-MOH-*lok*

PTEROSAUR –
TEH-*roh-sore*

DIMORPHODON –
die-MORF-*oh-don*

TRICERATOPS –
try-SERRA-*tops*

NYCTOSAURUS –
NIK-*toh*-SORE-*rus*

QUETZALCOATLUS –
kwet-zal-COAT-*lus*

RHAMPHORHYNCHUS –
RAM-*foh*-RING-*kus*

SORDES –
SORE-*deez*

PTERODACTYL –
teh-roh-DACT-*il*

IT'S 'UDDER' MADNESS!

Genius cow Professor McMoo and his trusty sidekicks, Pat and Bo, are star agents of the C.I.A. – short for COWS IN ACTION! They travel through time, fighting evil bulls from the future and keeping history on the right track...

When Professor McMoo invents a brilliant TIME MACHINE, he and his friends are soon attacked by a terrifying TER-MOO-NATOR – a deadly robo-cow who wants to mess with the past and change the future! And that's only the start of an incredible ADVENTURE that takes McMoo, Pat and Bo from a cow paradise in the future to the SCARY dungeons of King Henry VIII...

It's time for action.

MOO-SEY ON DOWN . . .

Genius cow Professor McMoo and his trusty sidekicks, Pat and Bo, are star agents of the C.I.A. – short for COWS IN ACTION! They travel through time, fighting evil bulls from the future and keeping history on the right track . . .

It's a GOLD RUSH! The C.I.A. have been sent back to the Wild West of America where a TER-MOO-NA-TOR and his shifty sidekicks are cheating the locals out of all the land they own. But why? With local cattle going MISSING and a sinister MONSTER on the loose, can Professor McMoo and his team solve their WILDEST case yet?

It's time for action.